"Did someone hurt you?"

Gabriella looked forward and focused on the trees swaying in the breeze, but it only served to remind her of the ticking clock. Twenty-four hours left until they killed her great-aunt, and she had no idea where to begin.

Who could she call? The police? The FBI? Absolutely not.

She moved to get out of the car. Luke stood to make room for her. He held out a hand to help her.

Normally, she'd wave it away, but as heavy as her bones felt she accepted. The strength in his grip as he gently pulled her to standing bolstered her determination. She would not let those men hurt her great-aunt Freddie—the woman had been like a second mother to her.

"Luke, it's not a good time to look at the property, after all. I'll call you to reschedule?"

Luke didn't flinch, and his hand didn't move from her wrist. "This isn't business. I'm here as a friend. My receptionist said you were arguing with that man before you left, and the black sedan followed you. What happened?"

Heather Woodhaven earned her pilot's license, rode a hot air balloon over the safari lands of Kenya, parasailed over Caribbean seas, lived through an accidental detour onto a black diamond ski trail in Aspen and snorkeled among stingrays before becoming a mother of three and wife of one. She channels her love for adventure into writing characters who find themselves in extraordinary circumstances.

Books by Heather Woodhaven

Love Inspired Suspense

Calculated Risk
Surviving the Storm
Code of Silence

CODE OF SILENCE

HEATHER WOODHAVEN

HARLEQUIN® LOVE INSPIRED® SUSPENSE

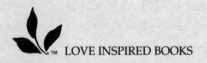

Recycling programs for this product may not exist in your area.

LOVE INSPIRED BOOKS

ISBN-13: 978-0-373-44736-7

Code of Silence

www.Harlequin.com

Printed in U.S.A.

Finally, brethren, whatsoever things are true, whatsoever things are honest, whatsoever things are just, whatsoever things are pure, whatsoever things are lovely, whatsoever things are of good report; if there be any virtue, and if there be any praise, think on these things.

–Philippians 4:8

To my husband, my critique group and to my editor, Emily Rodmell. Thank you for not being silent with your encouragement and ideas. You make these stories shine. And chocolate, you deserve some credit, too.

ONE

The shadow of a car darkened the patch of asphalt in front of her. Gabriella's neck tingled, and she held her breath. Everywhere she went, a black sedan crossed her path, as if following her.

Grief continued playing tricks on her mind.

The first few times she'd spotted the boxy-shaped vehicle, she'd thought she'd seen a hearse. She blinked. The car didn't so much as slow down as it passed by the parking lot and turned the corner, proving her thoughts to be ludicrous once again. No car—and definitely no hearse—was following her.

Gabriella pressed the papers she'd gathered against her chest and locked her car door. Instead of enjoying her summer break from teaching math at a junior high school, she needed to implore Luke McGuire for help. His voice had sounded as kind and smooth as ever on the phone when she'd scheduled the appointment, but she hadn't seen him since college, when their fiancés dumped both of them for each other. And a lot could change in eight years.

Gabriella ran her left palm against the side of her head in case any errant hairs had escaped the barrette.

As she approached the glass doors, she hoped the maroon peasant blouse, tan capris and navy flats looked professional enough for a visit to the real estate development office. She pulled the handle.

Luke McGuire stood in the lobby, addressing his receptionist. He wore a gray suit, white shirt and an azure tie that matched his blue eyes. She froze as they both turned toward her.

Luke's face fell. "Gabriella."

She let the door close behind her, and the air-conditioning sent an involuntary shiver up her spine. His expression confirmed her suspicions—seeing her just reminded him of the pain they'd experienced.

He held out a hand, and as she reached for it, she glanced at the hand by his side—no ring. Maybe he still hadn't gotten over his fiancée?

His brows furrowed. "I'm sorry to hear about your mom. I think I met her and your aunt once, at a parents' weekend. I remember because you two almost looked like—"

"Twins," she finished for him. Each time she looked in the mirror, the reminder of her loss hit her in the gut. Her throat fought against letting her words out. "She and my great-aunt came to every single one of those."

Luke turned and waved a hand toward the back. "Why don't we talk in my office?" He shortened his stride until she caught up. "Congratulations on the nonprofit, by the way. I saw you on the news last week when they announced their charity of the month."

Her shoulders relaxed at the change of subject, and she couldn't help but smile that Luke knew about the foundation she'd set up a few years back to help tutor struggling kids. "Oh. The grant took me by surprise. I didn't know anything about it until we showed up on the news."

She scrunched her nose. "I think they pulled my picture from the school staff website." Gabriella stiffened. What if Luke thought she was fishing for compliments? She rushed on. "Financially it's not a big grant, but the national media exposure is priceless. I'd be ecstatic, but—"

He nodded. "Of course. You're going through a lot right now."

Framed pictures of subdivision developments filled with cookie-cutter houses hung on the office walls. Her chest ached. Could she really go through with this?

As soon as he sat in his chair, she splayed the papers she'd brought with her across his desk. "I know you agreed to meet with me as a courtesy, but I really think the land has potential for one of the subdivisions you keep making." She hated the tremble in her voice but worried if she stopped she'd break down. "I brought a copy of the property map and printed out the county assessment of—"

"I'm sorry, Gabriella. I actually have all that information already. I gathered it after you called." Luke clasped his hands together. "I know it's getting late, but if you have time, I need a look at the property in person before we can discuss potential scenarios. I could follow you out there now."

"Wow. That's fast. It's good. It's what I need. Just fast." She nodded and continued nodding, processing his words. "I have time to show you around right now."

Luke clapped his hands together and jumped from his chair. "Perfect. I just need a moment to gather my camera and some paperwork. I'll be right behind you."

Gabriella took the cue and headed straight for the door. Her embarrassment at babbling coupled with his kindness would be her undoing. Her eyes burned with held-back tears. The moment she opened the door, heat slapped her in the face.

She squinted against the intense sunshine as a black sedan drove past the office. Was that really a different one than she'd seen moments before? Was she going insane? It, too, had darkened windows.

If it'd been a Subaru Outback, she would've had an easier time believing the coincidence. Many Idaho residents depended on the all-wheel drive, practically a requirement to living in Idaho. But a black sedan? She had no proof it was following her, though. The next time she spotted it, she'd make an effort to get its license plate number so she'd know for sure.

A man in a silver suit and navy dress shirt rounded the corner of the office building, smiling. She grinned in response, slightly amused at his greased-back hair. She'd only seen hair like that on New York models and wondered if he worked as a partner or employee for Luke. She stepped off the sidewalk and clicked the fob to unlock her car as the man passed.

She opened the car door. As it swung open, the man stepped next to her passenger door and wrenched it open. She clutched her purse. "Excuse me. What are you—"

He pulled his suit jacket back, revealing a gun holstered to his side. "Get in, Gabriella."

Gabriella's heart slammed into overdrive, and yet, she couldn't move. What did they say about people with guns? Never get in the car? Or, get in the car but drive into a building? She couldn't blink. Her vision focused on the gun. And how did he know her name?

"Don't be stupid. Look behind you."

Gabriella moved her chin ever so slightly. There was no way she was turning her back to the gunman. She peeked over her shoulder. The source of her insanity—the black sedan—pulled into the parking lot.

"Now see? It's not just me. And the guys in there aren't as nice." He stared at her with such intensity that she had to look away. "You wouldn't want other people getting hurt, would you?" he asked. "Not when you could be saving your great-aunt."

Despite the heat, everything turned cold. Gabriella's skin chilled. "What about her?"

Another man in a suit stepped out of the back of the black sedan and approached. He smiled, a grin that made her skin crawl. He nodded at the other man and opened the rear door of her car. "If I were you, I'd do everything he tells you. I'm not as patient."

"What'd I tell you?" the first gunman said. The men both laughed, sharing their own sick joke.

Gabriella's stomach twisted. She should've followed her great-aunt's advice and carried a gun or a brick in her purse. Even if she had, though, it'd be no match for the two men. And if they were telling the truth about Aunt Freddie being in danger, she couldn't risk it.

The second man loosened his suit jacket, and she spotted his gun, as well. She tightened her fists. "Is my aunt in that sedan? What'd you do with her?"

The man across from her turned and looked toward Luke's office. The sun bounced off the windows, so she couldn't see inside. *Please let Luke see something is wrong.*

"Do you want to see her alive again?" the first gun-man asked, his voice thick with a familiar accent she couldn't place.

She opened her mouth, her breath so ragged she wasn't sure she could answer if she tried. Aunt Freddie was her only living relative. It'd been hard enough to put her in assisted living last week—so hard Gabriella spent the past few nights sleeping on the couch at her new villa so Aunt Freddie wouldn't be lonely.

I can't lose her, too. Her gut dropped. The sedan following her the past few days…had she led them right to her aunt?

He smirked. "Get in and drive."

Luke hit the side of the printer, frustrated after two jams and irritated the temporary receptionist hadn't already finished the job. He didn't begrudge Deb her maternity leave, but he also selfishly prayed she didn't change her mind about coming back in six weeks. His sanity depended on it.

The motor whirred as the printer finally spit out his prize. He grabbed the paper, shoved it haphazardly into the leather satchel and strode for the door.

He hated keeping Gabriella waiting, especially since he had suggested the last-minute property tour. And since it was almost five o'clock already, he harbored hope she'd agree to have dinner afterward to catch up.

His mind replayed seeing her walk through his office door. She radiated a mixture of gentleness and beauty. And it made him angry with himself that he hadn't kept in touch. He'd meant to.

When he first settled on the Treasure Valley to start his business, his parents had challenged his sanity. But the economy was booming, and it turned out to be a smart move financially. If he was honest with himself, in the back of his mind he'd assumed Gabriella would've settled in the area, too. Instead, she accepted a job in a small town in Eastern Oregon but spent summers in the valley. He knew she stayed with her family and worked with her foundation director anytime she had a break from teaching. Yet he'd never reached out, though he'd meant to before now.

Even now his heart sped up at the thought of her, but he knew why he procrastinated. He'd put himself out there once before—albeit almost a decade ago—and been burned. He wanted to diminish the risk of repeating the scenario.

Gabriella had seemed pleased about the grant and the media exposure. So pleased, he'd been tempted to let her know he owned the responsibility for making it happen. But he took the Bible passage seriously that exhorted believers to give in secret.

Luke turned to the receptionist. "As soon as you're done with that file, you're free to go. You'll be paid for the full day. The door is set to lock behind you." He pressed the glass door open as he threw on his designer shades, a smile plastering his face. He loved summer. He stepped out to an empty parking lot.

He always parked behind the office building along with his employees. The spaces in front were reserved for clients. He grabbed the glass door before it fully closed. "Karen?"

"Yes?"

"Did you see where my client went?"

"Oh. Yeah." She picked at a piece of fuzz attached to her blouse. "She argued with some guy for a second, but then when she saw her friends coming, too, they like must have worked it out, 'cause they drove off together."

Luke rubbed the throbbing spot above his brow. "Her friends?" It didn't make sense. Gabriella was too considerate not to let him know she'd changed her plans. At least the girl he once knew would've been. Maybe she'd changed.

"Yeah, well I think so," Karen muttered. "Two of them got in her car and the others followed them when they left."

Luke's shoulders sagged. An impromptu reunion? He shook his head. It didn't add up. "Did she say anything when she left? Did she look upset?"

Karen lifted an eyebrow. "Well, yeah. Didn't you say her mom just died?"

Luke blew out a long breath. He spun on his heel and headed for his truck. Maybe Gabriella had changed her mind about putting the property up for sale, but if that proved to be the case, he still wanted to show her how serious he was about being her friend. And who was the guy she argued and left with? The back of his neck tensed.

People changed over the years, sure, but Gabriella's thoughtful nature defined her. Driving off without telling anyone didn't ring true.

He entered Gabriella's phone number and started his full-size Dodge Ram while it rang.

Four rings later it transferred to voice mail. Luke frowned. Something didn't sit well. He didn't want to be overly pushy, but he had also let Gabriella go once instead of being a true friend. He refused to make the same mistake twice. He shifted the truck into Drive and headed for Radcliffe Ranch.

TWO

Gabriella squeezed the steering wheel, but it didn't tame the tremors. Her entire body shook at the sight of Aunt Freddie on the tablet.

The video showed her aunt asleep, wearing a quilted blue robe, in a strange recliner with another suited gunman sitting next to her. "What'd you do to her? Where'd you take her?"

"Keep your eyes on the road." The man in her passenger seat clicked the tablet off. "She's been given a strong sedative. Doesn't even know that she went on a little field trip. And as long as you comply, she will be safe."

One lone car drove past her. She stared out the window, her eyes wide, hoping the driver would somehow see something was wrong. She didn't dare swerve, though, not with a madman watching her aunt sleep. "Who are you?"

The man grinned, sending shudders up her spine. "Benito." He shrugged. "Of the Mirabella family."

The way he said it…wasn't that how people referred to the mafia? A crime family?

"We're actually relatives," he said. "I'm your mother's second cousin."

"Me, too, twice removed." The man in the back chuckled. He sat in the middle, so that any time Gabriella looked in the rearview mirror she spotted his dark eyes, hard and void of compassion. She didn't want to know his name. If she did, it would surely haunt her dreams.

Gabriella forced herself to breathe. *Her mother's cousins?* It couldn't be possible. Her mom had no living relatives.

"You look just like Renata, by the way."

She turned to him, her mouth wide open. It was a mistake, a horrible mistake. She just needed to get them to see it. "You have the wrong person. I don't know a Renata. And my aunt struggles with dementia so she's no threat to you." She turned her clicker on and steered toward the side of the road. She'd let them out, promise to never tell a soul. Maybe they'd leave her and her great-aunt alone. *Please, Lord.*

"Nice try," the man named Benito said. "Stay straight, Gabriella. Your mother knew how to keep a secret. Impressive she kept it from her own daughter. Samantha was not your mother's real name, just like Frederica is not your great-aunt's name."

She clenched her jaw. Every muscle tightened as she pressed on the gas and regained speed. "If you actually knew them, you'd know they never let anyone address them like that."

"Ah, that's right. Only Sam and Freddie." He shook his head. "Very clever to use masculine names. If you hadn't made national news, we'd likely never have found you." He clucked his tongue in an annoying rhythm. "This ranch of yours is really in the middle of nowhere, isn't it? Believe it or not, I'm sorry to hear your mother passed. Her real name was Renata Mirabella. Your great-aunt is Amalia Mirabella."

Her stomach lurched. It had to be a lie and a dirty trick to make such accusations when her mother wasn't alive to defend herself. Her eyes burned, and her throat hurt to swallow. "What do you want?"

"Your mother made herself very useful to the family back in the day. She grew up helping out. She was your grandpa and great-uncle's favorite."

The man in back scoffed. "Shows how poor their judgment was."

Benito ignored him. "Eventually your mom handled the bookkeeping and served as a messenger between the bosses. Even snuggled up to the right people to help with some scores. After her father died, she disappeared, taking Uncle Claudio's wife—your aunt—with her. But she left a note. Said she had enough evidence to send most of the family to the chair. Upon her death, it would be delivered to the FBI. So we didn't chase her, on your great-uncle Claudio's orders."

Gabriella's foot slipped off the gas. Her mom had worked for the mob? No. Not possible. She shook her head. "I don't understand what it is you want from me."

"It's very simple. Get us the evidence, and we let you and your aunt go without consequence, out of respect for the family." He sighed. "I had a great fondness for your mother."

She blinked rapidly, trying to clear her vision as she turned down the long road that led to the ranch. She could see the wrought iron gates in front of the man-made lake. "You had a fondness for her? That's why you're holding her aunt hostage." The sarcasm kept her from leaping out of her seat and punching Benito in his smug face.

"I understand your mother didn't teach you the family business," he answered, his voice steady, "but affection only goes so far. If a relative turns on us, we turn on them. We do what it takes to protect the family." His chin jutted out. "Drive inside," he said.

Her shaky finger moved to the clicker. Her sanctuary, her safe place—she didn't want to let these crazy people in. The gate swung open as she turned in to the driveway. "But you don't understand. Even if you don't believe me that my mom never ran with the mafia, I'm telling you she didn't leave behind anything but this property. No evidence, no money…nothing! You could search the house and—"

"We already did," the gruff voice behind interrupted.

She inhaled sharply. What if she had slept at home the past week? What would they have done? She pulled her elbows in closer to her torso as she drove, wishing she could curl up in a ball, away from them.

"It's a big property," Benito said. "And your mom wouldn't be one to trust banks. Besides, we've already checked."

"So why kill ourselves trying to find it when you can do the work for us?" the man in back added.

"Even if you're right, which I promise you're not, why would you think the evidence hasn't already gone to the FBI?" She looked in her rearview mirror. The black sedan stayed behind her down the mile-long driveway that meandered through the property until they reached the house.

"If the FBI had it already, we wouldn't be having this conversation. Our sources think your mom left it for you." Benito winked. "Besides, we have connections. We would know if something was about to go down. But if that happened, it'd get…complicated for you and your aunt."

Gabriella pulled to a stop in front of the house but hesitated to shift into Park. The man in the back leaned forward, and through the rearview mirror she could see the way he leered. She kept one foot on the brake and one foot on the gas, in case he moved to try anything. At the very least she could drive into the lake.

"You have twenty-four hours, more or less," Benito said. "Depends on when the meds wear off on your auntie."

She gaped. "You can't be serious."

He stepped one foot out of the vehicle. "And if you feel tempted to call the police, we have people ready at a moment's notice to make sure your aunt never opens her eyes again."

"I'm telling you my aunt is no threat to you!"

He shrugged, unfazed. "We'd also need to alert someone to the fact the sizable anonymous donation your little foundation accepted last week came from a lawyer known to have ties with the Mirabella family. You may not know it now, but your grandfather and great-uncle made our name quite famous." He winked, left the car, straightened his jacket and bent down slightly. "We'll be in touch in twenty-four hours. Goodbye, Gabriella."

The man in the back stroked her cheek with the back of his hand. She flinched and pressed herself against the window. He laughed and joined his boss in the sedan.

Her bones ached as if they'd been filled with cement. How could this be happening? The black sedan

squeezed past her car and continued around the circu-
lar drive, past the lake. It disappeared behind the willow trees on its way back to the gate. A second later,
a navy Dodge Ram pulled up behind her. At the sign
of the shined wingtips, Gabriella shoved the car door
open. "Luke, get down."

His eyes widened, but he hunched over and looked
around.

"Stay there." Gabriella watched out the side window
as she saw glimpses through the foliage of the black
sedan nearing the gate. If they spotted Luke, there was
no telling what they would do, and she didn't want to
find out.

The sedan didn't seem to slow down, and since the
house wasn't visible from the road, maybe they were
in the clear. She held her breath a moment longer until
the vehicle disappeared from sight.

She exhaled and dropped her head. What was she
going to do?

"Are you okay?" Luke bent down to look into her
eyes.

Gabriella brushed the escaping tear away with the
heel of her hand. "Relatively speaking."

His eyes narrowed. "Who was in the black sedan?"

She shook her head.

"Did he threaten you?" His right hand rested on her
shoulder. "Gabriella, what happened? You're shaking
and pale."

She tried to force a smile. It was imperative he think
things were normal so she could convince him to leave.
"Thanks for the compliment." The attempted joke fell
flat, though, as her voice shook.

He narrowed his eyes. "Did someone hurt you?"

Gabriella looked forward and focused on the trees swaying in the breeze, but it only served to remind her of the ticking clock. Twenty-four hours left until they killed her great-aunt, and she had no idea where to begin.

Who could she call? The police? The FBI? Absolutely not. Her mother and aunt had told her a thousand times that for every ten good officers, a crooked one took a deal. And Benito's offhanded comments seemed to corroborate the sentiment.

She moved to get out of the car. Luke stood to make room for her. He held out a hand to help her.

Normally, she'd wave it away, but as heavy as her bones felt, she accepted. The strength in his grip as he gently pulled her to standing bolstered her determination. She would not let those men hurt her great-aunt Freddie—the woman had been like a second mother to her.

"Luke, it's not a good time to look at the property after all. I'm sorry I wasted your time. I'll call you to reschedule?"

Luke didn't flinch, and his hand didn't move from her wrist. "This isn't business. I'm here as a friend. My receptionist said you were arguing with that man before you left, and the black sedan followed you. What happened?"

The question caused her stomach to lurch as she remembered Benito's callous compartmentalization between business and family—if he even was actual family. She scoffed at the thought.

Luke's gaze dropped to her wrist. "Gabriella, your pulse is pounding against my hand." His blue eyes met hers as he flashed a smile. "And I don't think it's because of me." His expression sobered. "You either need to give me some hint of what's going on so I know you're safe or I'm calling the police and reporting that sedan for suspicious behavior."

He frowned and shook his head. "I haven't seen you look like this since…"

He didn't need to say it aloud. She knew he remembered the night they were dumped by their fiancés. Betrayed by those they loved.

"There's no need to call the police." Gabriella tugged her hand away from his touch. She couldn't think of an explanation that would keep him in the dark while he had a finger on the beat of her heart, but she also didn't want to lie to him. That was a nonnegotiable. She would never lie, and up until now, she thought her mother never did either.

"I am safe," she said. *At the moment.*

He tilted his head. "Gabriella?"

She melted when he said her name. "Yes?"

"Are you sure you're ready to sell?"

Oh, no. He thought she wanted to change her mind. But if she got her aunt out of this horrible situation, she'd still need Luke's help. She couldn't afford for him to think she was backing out.

She inhaled. This needed to be fast. "My mom's bank accounts didn't even hold enough money to cover the funeral costs. The property, as you know, is massive. And even though the deed is free and clear, I cleaned out my savings to pay for the property taxes that were due. My great-aunt has nothing to pay for her assisted living costs after September. I have no choice but to sell." Her eyes widened. "And I basically just told you I'm desperate."

He closed his eyes and his chin dipped. "I see why you would think that, but I didn't interpret it like that. I asked as your friend." He sighed. "But, if this property suits my needs, I promise to offer you a fair price. And I insist you ask other developers for bids."

"I came to you in the first place because I trust you."

He frowned. "Then what's the problem? Why'd you leave so fast if you hadn't changed your mind?"

This was the Luke she remembered. He never accepted simple answers. He always pursued the reasons and motivations until it made sense to him. Once, he followed their theology professor around and around the room, asking questions. He should've been a reporter. "I received some bad news about my great-aunt, and I need to make some unforeseen…arrangements."

He raised his left eyebrow. "Is this about the assisted living bills?"

She cringed. There he went, getting the wrong idea. She could see the pity in his eyes. "No. It's a private matter."

Luke crossed his arms across his chest, his strength evident as his biceps bulged against the suit jacket. "At least let me see you inside and make you a cup of tea. You look like you could faint."

She opened her mouth to protest, but he held out a hand. "You don't need to tell me any more if you don't want to, but I hope you know that I'm a great listener."

Unbidden memories sprang to mind: sitting together on a stone bench on campus after they'd just found out about their fiancés, organizing board game tournaments in the commons, studying at the library, laughing at the movie playing in the park. "I remember," she said softly.

If she argued against his kindness any more, he

would dig in his heels. Luke was as determined and stubborn as he was thoughtful and kind—probably why he succeeded in his career. She shrugged. "I have no idea what's in the pantry. I haven't been sleeping here, just stopping in on mornings to grab clothes."

She wanted to spend as little time as possible in the house. While it was not much easier to stay with her aunt in assisted living, coming home without her mother and aunt there proved too painful to endure.

He turned to face the front door. "We'll figure something out."

Luke looked up, gazing at the house her best friend from high school had once described as "a rich person's idea of getting back to nature." She agreed it made for an impressive sight. The luxury log cabin with tall windows and a brick foundation looked gorgeous in front of the backdrop of lakes, mountains and pine trees.

He led her to the front door. His arm shot out, blocking her path.

"What?" she asked. "What is it?"

"Did you lock the door when you left? It's slightly ajar." He pulled a phone from his pocket.

Her eyes darted to the door. She put a hand on his arm. "I'm sure you don't need to call the police." Benito said they'd already checked the house. But even if someone else had robbed all the contents, she wouldn't call the police until she got her aunt back.

"Don't you have a security system?"

It served as another reminder of a long list of things she couldn't afford. "I shut it down last week when I wasn't able to pay the bill." She closed her eyes, replaying the events of the morning.

Could she remember locking the door behind her?

"I was in such a rush this morning it's possible this is my fault. Not to mention I've been operating in a fog the past few weeks." She narrowed her eyes, trying to focus. "If you don't fully press in the lever on the handle when you close the door, it bounces back open."

His eyes widened. "Are you serious? You didn't lock it?"

"I locked it from the inside. When I'm running behind I don't usually lock the dead bolt. The gate locks, and we have barbed wire around the property." She pulled out her phone. "Which reminds me, I should lock the gate now."

She clicked in the access code, turned and squinted in order to see the gate's remote response in action. At the first sight of movement she headed up the front steps. "Let's get to that tea."

The faster she could down a cuppa, the faster she could hustle Luke out the door and focus on finding a solution to save her aunt. She pressed open the door and stepped inside.

The chairs in the entryway were slashed, bits of stuffing covering the marbled flooring. Why'd they need to go to such lengths? Surely they didn't expect to find something in the cushions of the chair. Had someone destroyed everything for the fun of it?

Luke's hand tugged on her shoulder. "I'm calling the police."

"I don't think so." A man dressed all in black strode around the corner. He lifted his right arm and aimed a gun at her chest. "We need to have a little chat."

Gabriella gasped as Luke stepped in front of her, shielding her. Another mafia member? Why was he here if they'd already searched the house?

Gabriella stared at the man's balding head, green eyes and five o'clock shadow. The gunman shook his weapon at Luke. "Get out of the way."

"I will not," Luke said.

While touched by his chivalry, she knew Luke would only escalate the problem. Gabriella's hand pressed into his back as her chin poked around his arm. "I thought I had twenty-four hours."

Luke's back stiffened under her fingertips. She'd let the cat out of the bag now. He knew she was keeping something from him.

Uncertainty crossed the gunman's features, but he blinked it away. "The timeline's been moved up," he said.

Her gut churned. If he wasn't on the same page as Benito, why was he here?

"Take what you want and leave," Luke said.

He scoffed. "I don't want your garbage." His eyes drifted to Gabriella. "I think she knows what I want."

So he *was* part of the mafia, then. Gabriella's throat tightened. "Benito didn't mention you."

He sneered. "Of course not. He's a punk with no manners. I'm Rodrigo Valenti. I worked for your uncle for years."

"As I told Benito, I never even met this so-called uncle."

He shrugged. "But your mama did. I heard all about it from your uncle before he passed."

All the talk of supposed relatives made her mad enough to almost forget about the gun. Almost. "Despite whatever you may have heard, I have no idea where this supposed evidence is. There's been a mistake. Mistaken identity. You have the wrong family."

He acted as though he didn't hear her. "I worked for your uncle Claudio for years, may he rest in peace, and he would've wanted you to give me the evidence instead of Benito."

Luke glanced at her over his shoulder, wide-eyed. She didn't know what to say. How had she ended up in the middle of what looked to be a mafia feud?

She pursed her lips, ready to launch into another rant about it all being a mistake and how she couldn't care less about some mysterious, fake uncle. But after two tries, she knew it'd do no good, and if she wanted to keep Luke safe, she might as well placate them. "Why would he have wanted me to give it to you?"

He waved his gun. "So I don't have to kill you."

THREE

Luke looked between the gunman and Gabriella, trying to make sense out of the situation. He clenched his fists and took a small step backward, trying to push Gabriella back outside, farther away from the gunman.

She worked against him, shoving herself forward so she was next to him instead of behind him. "Listen, please," she said. "Whoever gave you the idea my mother was involved in the mafia was way off. I...I can prove it. Let me find the deed. She inherited this land—no relation to any Mirabella family member."

Luke did a double take at the word *mafia*, but Gabriella avoided his gaze. This Rodrigo guy thought her mom had been part of the Mirabella mafia? That was absurd. They lived in a state with more cattle than people. Gabriella had the spunk, the dramatic flair and the Italian beauty associated with the famous crime syndicate, but she'd attended a Christian college and exhibited too much grace and kindness to ever—

She threw her hands up in the air. "And my mom worked in the sand and gravel mining business her entire life...in Idaho. That's the opposite of this mafia lady everyone keeps saying I look like. End of story."

Gabriella clasped her hands together. Her eyes glistened. "I told you exactly what I told Benito. You have the wrong person. I'm a Radcliffe, my mother was a Radcliffe and this is called Radcliffe Ranch. You can take anything you want in this house. Just go. Please go."

Rodrigo tilted his head as if considering her offer. "Twenty-four hours is too long. Forget Benito. New plan: you have twelve hours to get me the evidence."

Rodrigo stepped closer. Luke tensed his entire body so he'd be ready to knock away the gun if he got close enough.

"I wouldn't know where to start." Gabriella's voice cracked on the last syllable. "I have no idea what or where it would be." Her voice strengthened and rose in pitch. Luke wanted to pull her into his arms. This was too much. As if she didn't have enough grief and stress in her life, this man was trying to add more with his ridiculous mafia claim. No wonder Gabriella looked like death warmed over.

Rodrigo cackled. "Renata was a wily one, I'll give her that. She was your uncle's favorite until she disappeared." Rodrigo's cold stare moved Luke's way. His grin twisted as he pointed the gun toward Luke's forehead. "I don't need you."

The center of Luke's stomach turned to solid ice.

Gabriella threw her arms across his torso. "He knows this property. I've walked the land, but he's studied it. He's an expert, and he'd know possible hiding places I might not think of...and vice versa."

Rodrigo's lips pressed together in a thin line, but his gaze never wavered. Luke wasn't about to let him win the staring contest, even though the cavernous room with vaulted ceilings was sure to be echoing his loud heartbeat.

Rodrigo waved the gun toward the door. "I want a tour of the property. Now. But first, drop your keys and phones."

Luke exhaled and tossed his phone on the closest bunch of ripped padding in hopes it wouldn't break. If they could lose the creep somewhere on the property, they could get back to the house and call the police.

Gabriella was more graceful, bending down and setting the phone right in front of her feet. Surely she wasn't going to try to get Rodrigo close enough to take him out? Luke tried to get her attention by bending his head down with wide eyes. She just glanced at him and shrugged.

Heat rushed to his legs. He wasn't about to let Gabriella make the first move. He shifted his feet, ready to pounce if Rodrigo got too close.

"Slide it over, princess."

Gabriella pressed her lips together as she kicked the phone in Rodrigo's direction. So much for that plan.

Rodrigo put the keys in his pocket and picked up the phones as well. "Lead the way."

The moment they stepped onto the driveway, their phones soared above their heads and landed with a plop in the lake.

There went three hundred bucks. He knew he should've waited before upgrading.

"Take me to your mom's favorite spots," Rodrigo growled.

Gabriella made a sharp turn to the right, her flats slapping on the concrete and her hands in fists. Luke matched his step with hers.

"I should've gone with my gut and called the police while I had a chance," Luke whispered. "Any landline or other cell phone inside?"

"No. And calling the police isn't an option."

Luke put a hand on her arm. "Care to fill me in?"

She kept her face forward as she spoke. "Those men you saw me with earlier—in the driveway—are from the mafia, as well. They've got my aunt Freddie and will kill her if I don't get them this mysterious evidence."

"The same evidence Rodrigo wants?"

She nodded. "He acts like he's in the same group as them, but he clearly doesn't know or care about my aunt. We have to get away from him."

Luke replayed the events of the past few minutes. Ah, it had to be the reason for her careful wording: *I received some bad news about my great-aunt.* Rodrigo was still far enough away he wouldn't be able to hear his whispers. "The police are more capable of saving her than you are."

Her dark eyes flashed. "The police can't get involved. You can't trust them."

"Says who?" Luke frowned. His own mother had been a police detective before she retired, and he'd trust her with his life. Okay, so maybe he was a little biased.

"Too much corruption. I was taught never—" Her eyebrows shot up. "That's not normal, is it? At school they want us to tell the kids to find an officer when they're in danger. It would be just like a mafia family to teach you not to trust law enforcement." She shook her head as if flinging the thoughts away. "Still, not worth the risk. Benito said he had connections. He said he'd know. Besides, it's a moot point."

"You better be talking about possible places for

my evidence," Rodrigo barked. "Otherwise, shut your yaps."

Rodrigo was ten paces behind them, looking around but keeping the gun trained on Luke's back.

Luke reached for Gabriella's hand and squeezed it. "Thanks for selling my worth back there."

Her eyes widened. "I meant every word. You said you did your homework on this property, and I need all the help I can get to stay alive…and somehow save my aunt."

Luke tried to picture the topographical map he'd studied that morning. "That's a tall order."

"We have to get away from Rodrigo. Benito will kill my aunt in twenty-four hours if I don't cooperate. I can't waste a single minute." She kicked at a pebble and watched it soar across the lush grass. "Who knew a math-tutoring program would bring mobsters to my door?" She laughed, but it came out garbled like a choked cry.

A heavy weight settled in the pit of Luke's stomach. "Wh-what do you mean, your program brought them to your door?"

"The national attention from the media…my picture. That's how these men said they found me."

Luke's insides turned to lava. This was his fault? He tried to do something nice for her, and instead he'd brought danger to her doorstep? "Uh, Gabriella—"

"I want some answers," Rodrigo shouted.

"My mom liked to walk around the lake," she said loudly. "Maybe we'll see something on the beach portion."

Rodrigo grunted and jutted his chin out as a sign to continue.

"You have almost two hundred acres," Luke said.

"Yes, but water accounts for more than half of it. We've got the lake and three tributaries."

"Basically an urban island, I'm aware. Do you know how long it would take to check out all the land on foot? He's asking us to go on a wild-goose chase—" he stepped over a spattering of goose droppings "—of which the property clearly has no shortage. But you get my point."

Her head dropped. "I…I can't think of a single spot that would be obvious as a place she'd hide something, let alone a place for evidence. They think she would've kept it close to her."

Rodrigo seemed to have no trouble letting them talk as long as they were discussing the property.

"He said he already searched the house." Gabriella lowered her voice. "But she kept a gun and a journal in her nightstand. Those have to help us."

Luke didn't think finding a journal was a high priority, but he didn't want to argue with Gabriella in this state. The gun was worth going after, and their only hope. "So we're agreed the first thing we do is get away from this guy and get back to the house."

She didn't reply, but Luke took that as agreement. He'd noticed when he pulled up in the driveway that there was a second driveway leading to the back of the house where a shed was built. A shed usually meant tools.

Luke waved toward the lake that wrapped around the south and west sides of the house—providing an almost three-hundred-degree view. The steady breeze sloshed miniature waves up on the shore. "You said it was a man-made lake. Did your mother have it built?"

Luke stopped for a moment, allowing Rodrigo to catch up enough to hear his words.

Gabriella squinted. "Yes. She mined the whole property for sand and gravel, then had it built back up to create the water features."

Rodrigo's forehead wrinkled, but he said nothing.

Luke addressed him. "What are you going to do if it turns out her mom buried something underneath this lake? Or one of the creeks?"

"Just keep walking," Rodrigo spat back, but his eyes were on the lake.

Luke tried to keep his smug grin to himself. He'd accomplished his mission to get the guy thinking and worrying over something so he'd be less focused. Luke put a hand on his chest and made a small gesture with his thumb for only Gabriella to see. "Let's make a sharp turn there," he whispered, "and make a run for it."

Her eyes widened. "But he has a gun."

Luke glanced over his shoulder and gauged the man's fitness level. His sizeable mass meant he probably didn't have endurance but could very likely have speed. "Then we pick up the pace. We'll have two…maybe three seconds at most. I'll get behind the shed and try to knock the gun out of his hands when he passes. Go in front of me. There's a back door, right?"

"Yes."

"Don't wait for me. Don't turn back. Go past the shed and get inside the house." Luke figured this was their best and only shot at getting the gun away from the man. If they walked any further they'd start dealing with uneven terrain and little to no shelter from Rodrigo.

If he succeeded, he'd get his keys back and haul him straight to the police.

Her face paled, but she did pick up the speed ever so slightly. Luke inhaled, and one of his mother's favorite phrases came to mind. *Remember: bravery is just doing what's right even when it's scary or hard.* Luke hoped the line between bravery and foolishness wasn't too thin.

Gabriella reached the corner and launched off her back foot into a sprint. She'd taken off too soon. Luke winced and glanced back. She was supposed to have waited until she rounded the corner.

Rodrigo raised his gun. "Hey!"

Luke dashed to the shed—Gabriella had already passed—and grabbed a shovel leaning up against the open door. Rodrigo rounded the corner. Luke flipped the shovel in a high arc, aiming for the gun. Except Rodrigo pointed the weapon, moving his arm. The metal blade hit Rodrigo's elbow. He howled, and the gun flew backward.

Rodrigo spun and took off after the gun.

"Luke!"

He turned to the sound of Gabriella's voice. She beckoned him. He ran toward her. There was no way he could beat or overcome Rodrigo's bulk. "Go!" He didn't want Gabriella waiting for him. Instead of running toward the back door of the house, she ran in the opposite direction onto a small wooden pier.

"Trust me," she hollered. Her arms stretched above her head as she pushed off from the dock and disappeared into the water below.

Crack!

Luke covered his head with his hands, but his legs

pressed harder and faster forward. He leapt off the pier where he thought he'd seen Gabriella dive. He hoped it was deep enough. As he sliced through the water, a searing hot pain ripped through his thigh.

FOUR

Gabriella's lungs burned as she did her best to stay at the bottom of the lake. As an only child she'd developed some unusual skills with all the time alone. She had, for instance, challenged herself to hold her breath for as long as possible every summer.

Her personal best was three minutes, though she'd never imagined it to be useful.

A strong current shoved the hair in front of her face. It had to be Luke. She kicked, swimming forward, until her fingertips touched fabric. While it was hard to see him through the murky water, his limbs flailed. His right arm bumped into her shoulder with a force that almost made her gasp.

Was he drowning? If he panicked, he could take her down with him. She grabbed the back of his suit jacket. It allowed her to stay far enough away he couldn't smack her as she tugged. She needed to breathe!

She tugged again, and he stopped fighting her. Her chest seized. She wasn't going to last much longer. The sunlight disappeared. With a final strong kick, she lifted her chin and took a hungry breath underneath the pier. Her heart pounded in her throat. Her temples throbbed.

The slightest light between the slats of decking high-lighted the eight inches that separated the underside of the dock and the lapping water. Her nose almost touched the wood as she sucked in another breath. Luke's head popped up so forcefully his forehead hit the wood.

Please don't let Rodrigo have heard that.

He hacked, coughed and greedily gasped before hacking some more. Gabriella cringed. She straightened. Her toes dragged against the sand. "Try to stand up," she whispered. "It's not as deep here. I'm not tall enough, but I imagine you are. Lift your hands up to help you breathe."

He coughed up more water. He reached up and grasped the space between the planks with the fingertips of his right hand.

Water poured in several streams from the sleeve of his suit. She needed to get that off him. Gabriella tugged on his left arm. His eyes met hers, and he twisted around, apparently understanding her motive. His breathing grew regular once she'd freed him.

She balled up the fabric in her hand. Slapping feet vibrated the planks. Her heart rate sped as Luke stilled. Gabriella glided next to him. She pressed her cheek against his cold, wet skin and whispered directly into his ear, "Stay here."

He nodded and muffled his coughing into his elbow. Gabriella hated to go underwater again. Her lungs still hurt, and the strong fish smell wafting off the water didn't help matters.

She expanded her rib cage as wide as it could go, then sank down low. Her toes pushed off from the sand as she used the dolphin kick to move as far away as her breath would allow. She dove down as close to the bottom as possible, dropped the suit jacket, spun around and kicked hard, back to the deck.

Two seconds later, muffled gunshots pierced the water. Even though she knew she was likely far enough to be safe, each one still gave her a jolt. She kept her hands out in front of her until she saw the lighted pattern from the slats.

Before her head was fully out of the water she inhaled deeply. The pounding overhead retreated. Her trick had worked. Rodrigo thought Luke had shed his jacket and was swimming away. Or dead after the shots. But since he wouldn't see a body floating, he'd likely think they were still alive and trying to escape the property.

She could hear him running away. *Thank You, Lord.*

Ten feet away, Luke had his arms wrapped around a pole that led to the lake floor. She used the breaststroke to join him.

"That was good thinking." He kept his voice low and moved his lips close to her hair. "I don't think he believed you that I was that valuable. Notice he didn't shoot at you."

"I wasn't the one who hit him with a shovel." She pressed the wet hair away from her face. "Doesn't mean he wouldn't shoot me now. Surely he gets the point. We don't know where the evidence is. Let's just pray he moves on."

Luke shivered, his teeth chattering. "Were you hoping to wait him out under here?"

"Not for long. The reeds are all along the water's edge. We can use it as camouflage to get back to the house. Are you okay? Are you able to swim and follow me?"

"I think so. I can't get a good look at where he shot me, but I'll do my best to keep up."

Her jaw dropped. "He shot you? Are you okay? Where?"

"In the leg. I can still move it, though, so maybe it's just a graze."

"Or adrenaline." She closed her eyes. All she wanted was to get him away from danger, not make things worse. "I'm so sorry, Luke. I just reacted without thinking. I knew the farther we got away from him the less accurate his shot would be but—"

"You were trying to get away from the shooter. I get it. Why the change of plan, though? Why not go into the house?"

"No keys, remember? The back door was locked. Ironic, right?" The waves grew bigger and slapped against the pole. Her ears perked. She held up one finger to her mouth. Had Rodrigo hopped in?

She needed to stick to the plan and get Luke's wound treated as soon as possible. "Can you keep your hand on your wound? I don't know how much good it would do but we don't know how much blood you're losing."

Thankfully she'd spent every single summer swimming this lake and could visualize the layout with her eyes closed. She'd even dreamed about it during the long winters.

Gabriella pressed off from the pole and glided to the next one six feet away. She beckoned Luke to follow. He tried to swim toward her while keeping his hand on his leg. His uncoordinated movements made a few waves that splashed against the other poles. Gabriella tensed and listened for signs Rodrigo had heard him.

The wind produced ripples across the surface. *Please let him think it's just the wind.*

The intensity of swimming underwater waned and as her heart rate slowed, the chill of the early summer waters produced goose bumps up and down her arms. She clenched her jaw and repeated the floating technique.

The reeds began at the end of the dock. It was the perfect place to catch bass—the lake was stocked with both bass and rainbow trout—and though it made a good hiding place, it would be uncomfortable. They'd have better agility if they kicked off their shoes, but they'd likely need the protection when navigating the woody, prickly plants. She hated to think of just how many fishing hooks she'd lost over the years within those reeds. They hid there, lurking, waiting to poke them.

She placed her palm on top of the water and waited for Luke to accept her hand. Together they slipped into the first bunch of reeds, careful to keep their bodies submerged.

The sensation was akin to hiding in a wet hay bale—not that she'd ever done that—and she just wanted out as soon as possible. Something slimy slipped past her arm. She released a silent squeal as she squirmed closer to Luke.

He raised his eyebrows.

"Hoping that was a fish," she whispered. "Do you see Rodrigo?"

Luke pointed to the west. "He's running alongside the lake, toward the willow trees."

"Good. He probably thinks he's going to cut us off before we get to the gate."

"Agreed, but if we're not careful he'll still see us.

We'll need to take it slow." Luke lifted his hand to wipe his hair away from his face, but he froze when he saw the blood on his palm.

His face paled, and he plunged his hand back into the water to apply pressure to his leg.

Taking it slow meant less risk of Rodrigo spotting them, but Gabriella couldn't afford that luxury. The summer sun didn't dip below the horizon until ten o'clock in June, but her rumbling stomach told her it was already past dinner. Her chance to save her aunt and Luke was slipping away.

They wordlessly swam together, their heads just above water, uncomfortably close to the border of the reeds lest they needed to hide at a moment's notice. Swimming proved more difficult in her clothes. Her shirt kept catching on the woody stems.

The lake wrapped around the house, so Gabriella figured they could get as close to the front door as possible before leaving their hiding place. Luke's teeth finally stopped chattering, either from the exercise or from going into shock. Either way, she wanted to get him inside as fast as possible. She barely registered the cacophony of nature around her. The toads croaking, the crickets in the distance…

In the sunlight, she really wanted a chance to look at Luke's wound but knew that would make them more vulnerable to being seen.

"You keep looking at me like that, you're going to give me a complex," he muttered.

Gabriella smiled. "I wanted some heads up if you were going to pass out on me."

He shrugged. "I'm made of tougher stuff than that." His eyes widened, and he grabbed her shoulder. She froze as something glided out of the reeds. Her breath caught. With two beady eyes and an open mouth swinging side to side, the snake's long body slithered mere inches in front of her face. A bright white line on top made it impossible to stay still. Poisonous snakes usually had stripes and colors. She kicked backward into Luke's chest.

"It's just a garter snake," he whispered.

Gabriella's heart didn't seem to register his reassurance because it continued to speed up. "Are you sure? I thought those were supposed to be small. This one is like four feet long."

"I'm positive. Your property must feed it well."

A moment later they'd reached the shore nearest to the driveway. "I'll keep a watch out while you climb out. If you go right between our cars and stay low, we should be safe from view. Theoretically."

Luke frowned. "I think you should go first."

"No offense, but you are injured and likely to take longer to get out."

His blue eyes locked on hers but she couldn't begin to imagine what he was thinking.

"Then we go together," he said.

"Fine." It actually made more sense since she could help him out. The muddy climb proved challenging. She fell to her knees twice, and dirt slipped underneath her fingernails. "This is the reason there's a ladder attached to the dock in the back." Streams of water poured off her blouse and her stringy hair as she tugged on Luke. Her left foot slipped, and she fell back into the grass, the breath knocked out of her.

Luke fell to his knees. "Maybe we should crawl."

She took a shuddering breath, her lungs refilling.

She scanned the property for Rodrigo. So far no sign, but it'd be far easier for him to see them from the trees without them spotting him. Her temples throbbed. She did as Luke suggested and turned to crawl.

The moment her fingers touched asphalt, she got to her feet but crouched down. That's when she saw it—the rip, the gash and the blood dripping from Luke's pants. All that time in the lake and brushing up against the reeds likely increased the chance of infection, as well.

Luke's face paled as he followed her gaze. "Not good with blood," he croaked and fell to his knees.

FIVE

"Luke!" She put both hands on his face. The contact grounded her, gave her a new focus. "Keep looking up. Don't you dare pass out on me."

He blinked in reply.

"Just keep moving." She darted past the vehicles and to the door. She peered at the thick grove of trees to her right. Her eyesight wasn't the best with long distances, so it didn't mean he wasn't watching.

Luke hobbled, bent over until he reached the stoop. The door remained ajar from their last exit at gunpoint. It swung inward to the same mess as before, except now they created puddles all over the marble and clumps of batting all over the floor. She closed the door behind him. "Be careful. The marble gets slippery when wet."

"Make sure you lock it."

"Uh…okay," she answered and clicked the dead bolt. "You do know he has my keys though, right?"

His lips sloped into a half grin. "I've been shot."

"So take it easy on you, got it." She picked up his left hand and draped it over her shoulder while placing her right arm around his back.

"I appreciate what you're doing, but it's not necessary."

Gabriella dropped his arm and stepped to the side. "Right." She didn't miss the sensation of his arm pressed onto her already sticky, wet clothes. Still, she wondered if he was trying to give her a signal not to get close. Because even macho men who were shot took help when they needed it, right? Of course she wouldn't know. She hadn't grown up with a man in her life.

Gabriella took the curved staircase two steps at a time until she reached the top. She stopped abruptly to check on Luke when he bumped into her back. She looked over her shoulder. "Sorry. I didn't think you could keep up with me."

His face paled and his eyes widened as he tipped backward.

"No!" Her fingers grabbed his dress shirt as she threw her body weight in the opposite direction in hopes he didn't take her down with him.

He grabbed the banister and regained his balance. "Sorry. I got dizzy."

"You've probably lost more blood than we realized." Her stomach twisted at the thought. First aid had never been her strong suit. As a teacher she carried the required certifications, but it was a lot easier to perform on a dummy than a real live person.

If Luke passed out or worse, she had no idea what she would do.

Luke followed Gabriella into a posh master bedroom. The sheets and drawers thrown on the ground proved it'd been ransacked. The room held a king-size bed with a matching armoire, end tables and desk. Even with all the furniture, it still left ample room for the entertainment center and a high-end treadmill. The bedroom alone looked to take up a third of the upstairs floor. If his leg wasn't throbbing, he'd have whistled.

Gabriella groaned. "No, no, no." She ran to the nightstand and sorted through the drawers. "He took it. He took my mom's gun." She straightened with a leather-bound book in her hands. Her eyes wild, her hair matted, she stared at him. "Luke, I had no idea, but I should've known. I'm not thinking straight."

"It's hard to think straight when your life is in danger." He should know. He'd already demonstrated that more than once in the past thirty minutes.

She shook her head. "I've gotten us into an even worse situation. We have no weapon to help us get out of here."

A slam punctuated the end of her sentence. They had company. A holler from below followed by a thump and a bellow of rage tempted Luke to walk back out into the hallway to see what was going on.

Gabriella crossed the room and grabbed his arm. "I told you that marble is slippery when wet." She gestured with her head. "Get into the closet."

"The closet?"

"I know you're in here!" A shot rang out, and Luke jumped back two feet. A hole appeared in the drywall one inch from the doorjamb.

"Now." Gabriella gave him a shove and they stepped into what he assumed was her mother's walk-in closet. She grunted as she closed the door and clicked the top dead bolt. Two more dead bolts—one in the middle and one near the ground—also needed to be flipped. Dead bolts in the closet?

"Get the other door, Luke."

On the opposite side of the closet was an open doorway attached to a lavender room complete with a queen-size bed underneath a floral canopy. Luke worked to close the door. The outside layer looked like normal wood, but the cool feel and heft meant it had to be metal. He engaged the three dead bolts then stood, hands on his hips. His leg progressed from a sore pounding to a sharp stinging.

"It connected to my room," she explained.

He gritted his teeth. It'd do no good to complain about the pain. "I hate to break it to you, but this isn't the best hiding place." He hobbled into the adjoining bathroom. Odd. The only door to the bathroom was inside the closet. The inside walls looked like white metal. "There's no window in here." He turned to Gabriella. Great. A madman outside and no means of escape. "We're trapped."

A small current of cold air rushed past his face. The air-conditioning had kicked on. Gabriella crossed her arms over her chest and shivered. "I know. It's a safe room. I didn't want to be responsible for you getting shot a second time."

He'd heard safe rooms were becoming more common, but he'd never been in one so ample—although not counting the bathroom, at only ten foot by ten foot in size it wouldn't take long to feel claustrophobic. "Is there a phone? Surveillance cameras?"

Her head dropped, and her damp hair fell in ringlets across her shoulders. "No. I already told you. Only cell phones. We used to have surveillance—" she pointed to a small tablet on top of the dresser "—but that was part of the alarm service, and they took back their cameras when I had to cancel." She turned away from him and placed a hand on the white door. "At least—"

Crack!

Gabriella screamed and stepped back into his arms. Her knees buckled, and Luke strained to hold her up until she regained her balance. He squinted at the pointed bulge in the door. That had been too close for comfort.

Gabriella rubbed the spot underneath her collarbone where it would've hit had it gone through. Luke's stomach churned at the thought. He kept a hand on her back as they stared at the bulge.

"My mom told me she made this room for tornadoes."

His heart pounded against his chest. The only sounds in the room were his heart and ragged breathing. Three more cracks and three more bulges appeared in the door. He flinched at each one. Gabriella's back pressed against his chest. He placed his hands on her arms and finally exhaled, not realizing he'd unintentionally held his breath. "Tornadoes are rare in Idaho."

She lifted her face up, toward him. "I know. I realized it in high school. I thought she was my overprotective mom. I never imagined—" Her voice broke and she stepped away from his support.

Another coughing spell hit him. His lungs still burned from inhaling the lake water after the bullet hit him. He glanced down at the wound. Blood wasn't gushing, but it still needed to be addressed. He turned his eyes back to the ceiling in hopes there wouldn't be a return of the dizziness that claimed him the last time he saw the wound.

Gabriella followed his gaze. "I'm glad Mom attached a bathroom. There used to be a first-aid kit somewhere."

Luke followed her into the spacious bathroom.

She handed him a red canvas bag from inside the bathroom closet. "At least we know the walls will hold for a little bit. Until we figure something out." She pulled out a thick terry-cloth towel and wrapped it around her shoulders. "Wait a second." She darted into the closet and returned with a stack of jeans and a flannel shirt. "My mom bought baggy men's clothes for when she had to supervise the gravel pits. I don't know if any of these will fit you but—"

Luke eagerly accepted the clothes. "We can always hope." He lifted his chin. "A minute ago you were holding a book. What was it?"

"Mom's diary." She turned around, looking at the floor. "I'm pretty sure I dropped it the moment we stepped in the closet. There it is." She raised her fingers to her temples and pressed. "I'll close this door and give you some privacy. I'm sorry I got you into this whole mess, but I'd be lying if I said I wasn't glad you were here."

"You couldn't make me leave your side if you tried." He meant it, but his words triggered the memory of their previous conversation. He needed to tell her he was behind the media spotlight. He was responsible for this mess, not her.

Would she ever be able to look at him again if she knew it was his fault these men had found her? But as the water and blood dripped on her bathroom floor, it probably wasn't the best time to share that information.

"I'll hurry," he said. "You start going through the

diary. We may be safe, but we're also trapped. We need to figure out how to escape before Rodrigo gets any bright ideas."

Four more muffled gunshots produced bulges on the steel door leading to her childhood bedroom. Gabriella screeched and pressed herself up against the bathroom door.

"You okay?" Luke hollered.

"I'll be better after he gives up." She blew out a long breath and tried to relax her muscles, but they refused to release the contraction, most likely because she couldn't stop shivering from the cold. She held her breath, listening. Rodrigo was either gathering more bullets or thinking up a new plan. The smell of cedar and mothballs permeated the room now that the doors were closed. If they decided to try to make a run for it, she would at the very least like dry clothes.

She crossed the room and stood in front of the dresser. The drawers stuck out slightly. The mafia men must have gone through them as well. Was there nothing of her mother's that they hadn't manhandled? She rubbed her hands together. Her throat throbbed with the strain it took to keep the tears at bay. She could do this.

Gabriella reached out tentative fingers and pulled out the top drawer. Her mother's shirts. She pulled out one and pressed it up against her face. The scent of flowers simultaneously soothed her and made her eyes burn.

Her mother loved the vanilla-and-lavender fabric softener, but Gabriella feared she'd never be able to use it without thinking of her.

She opened her eyes and spotted a gold paper box

still sealed up in cellophane—her mother's favorite brand of dark chocolate caramels. Gabriella remembered sneaking into the closet—her mom insisted on keeping the doors open—during a few late nights as a child to snitch a caramel before diving back in bed with a flashlight and a book. Her mother always knew, though. It was easy to count the chocolates. As if on autopilot, Gabriella unwrapped and stuck a chocolate in her mouth.

The door behind her slid open. "What are you doing?" He stepped out in a light-blue-and-navy striped flannel shirt and carpenter jeans that looked too tight. At least they were dry, though.

"Stress eating," she mumbled and popped another one in her mouth.

He raised his eyebrows and reached out for one. "Oh. Dark chocolate."

"The only good kind," she muttered and replaced the box lid. "Were you able to patch yourself up?"

He moved to the rod and shoved the hanging clothes apart. "Getting dry helped a lot and I found Steri-Strips. It'll have to do." He placed his hand on the back of the closet and glided his hand across the wooden surface.

"What are you doing?"

"Looking for an exit, or panel for a phone, or something that will help us out! Your mom went to the trouble of making this safe room because she feared something might happen." He threw a thumb over his shoulder. "At least we know she picked one paneled with Kevlar."

Gabriella rifled through the dresser and pulled out a green cotton blouse. "She used to have an alarm security system. I'm not sure she thought she'd have to get out of here without help." She pointed to the red button above the top shelf. "I had no idea her neurotic over-protective nature was justified."

She dropped to her knees and pulled out the lower drawer. Her mom used to keep her "skinny days" clothes at the bottom. Gabriella pulled out the acid-washed denim. "You know, I don't even know how to think of her anymore—was she Samantha or Renata?"

Luke stilled. "She was your mom. For now, that's all that matters."

"I know that," she snapped and instantly regretted it. The back of her neck heated. "Sorry." She bit her lip and stood. "Find us a way out while I change." She closed the bathroom door behind her. She didn't want to think about her mother any longer. Her ribs literally hurt, as if they couldn't handle the concave hole in her heart. She needed to focus on a way out. She hastily changed. It was a relief to have warm and dry fabric on again.

She opened the door to find Luke with her mother's diary. He held it out. "I think we need to start reading. It's possible she had some backup scenarios already planned if the mafia ever came looking for her...for you. If it's too painful for you, then I can read it aloud."

Gabriella's fingers touched the smooth leather. "No, I will."

A high-pitched squeal, though stifled, sent a chill up her spine. "Luke?"

"I hear it." She held her breath as they listened to-gether. A horrible grinding noise seeped through the walls and abruptly stopped. "I think he's trying to drill through the doors," he whispered. "These walls are so thick, though, it'd take him hours. Sounds to me like he drilled at high speed and snapped the bit. To drill through metal you need to go at a low speed."

She could feel her eyes widen. "I'll read fast."

"And I'll keep looking for an escape."

She sank to the ground, taking care not to sit on a previous wet spot. The whir of the drill started again.

"What kind of tools did your mom own?" Luke asked. "What are we dealing with?"

"I don't know, and I don't want to think about it. It's hard enough to focus on reading my mom's journal without reminders that we're really not safe in the safe room."

His lips formed a grim line. "Understood."

That feeling she remembered from college returned. Peace, even if temporary, relaxed her shoulders. Luke had a way of making her feel like she was acting reasonable, even when logically she knew she wasn't. He listened…he empathized. He made her feel calm despite the storm surrounding her. "Thank you," she said. "If I remember anything, I'll say."

He gave her an encouraging grin. She opened to the first page. Her mother's familiar script lined the pages.

I'm so hopeful to give this baby the life she deserves. At church today they read a Bible verse in Philippians about forgetting about the past and pressing on. There was more to it, but just the reminder that I can leave my past behind and focus on my future as a mom gives me hope. Maybe I can be the woman—the mom—God desires me to be, even though if you'd asked me a year ago I would've thought it impossible.

Gabriella's fingers drifted across the page. "I've read this before."

"You have?" Luke lifted his arms while raised on his tiptoes and grabbed a plastic storage container. He lowered it to the ground and faced her. A sudden high-pitched growl erupted from the other side of the wall. His eyes widened. "I can't imagine how loud that had to be out there if we can hear it through the steel."

"Another broken drill bit?"

"That'd be my guess." He dropped to a knee and flipped the latches holding the top of the container down. "You've read your mother's diary before?" he asked again.

"Yes." Her cheeks heated. Nothing like revealing every horrible thing about herself, and her family, to a guy. "But I think she knew I peeked sometimes. All her entries are very vague except for the scriptures she loved. Those she'd go on and on about in detail. Or at least she did early on in it." Her eyes lingered on her mom's first words, wishing she could have the woman who penned them. Her eyes welled. "I thought she wrote about the Bible verses for my benefit. Except, now if it's true…if my mom had a life in the mafia—" She stopped and pressed a hand to her closed eyelids. She wouldn't let herself cry. "It has a different meaning."

"We don't know that yet. Don't give up hope."

The sound of the lid popping open snapped her out of it. "What's in there? More clothes?"

Luke grinned as he reached inside. "A flashlight, bottled water—" he tossed a twenty-ounce bottle to her "—blankets, granola bars." He frowned and pulled out a dangling Pinocchio wooden puppet and a ten-inch doll dressed in a traditional Sicilian costume. "Were these yours?"

Gabriella moved to a kneeling position. "I think they used to be my mom's toys, but I did play with them once."

He pulled out a canister of pepper spray, his expression hopeful. "You think this still works?"

She reached past his outstretched arms and picked up a granola bar. "Check the expiration date."

He twisted the can and squinted at the small print. "Three years old."

"Then, no."

He gave her a side glance. "I can't imagine it wouldn't still be effective even after the expiration date."

"Oh, it'd still be potent, but that's not the problem. It's the aerosol spray part. After the expiration, there is a higher probability it'll get clogged." She opened the wrapper to the bar. "Not worth the risk. The last thing we need is to pepper spray ourselves."

She could feel his eyes studying her. "How'd you know that?" he asked.

"Mom sent me with pepper spray to college. She never did anything without making sure she had all the facts. She was the queen of preparation, and she made sure I was, as well." The metal screeching sound started up again. She jerked and accidentally brushed against his arm. The touch made her long for a hug, but she didn't want to send mixed signals—or worse, open herself up for rejection. No doubt he was wishing she'd never stepped into his office. "Clock is ticking, Luke. We need to get out of here."

"I'm aware." He ran a hand through his still-damp

golden hair. It spiked up. "I've checked the walls and the tops of the shelves. I don't know what else we can do."

Her stomach grew hot and heavy as if her veins pumped molten lead. "You're not implying we should give up and wait to die? To let my aunt die?"

SIX

Luke gritted his teeth. An unseen vacuum in his chest made his rib cage seem hollow with the pure frustration of not being able to fix things. His memory taunted him with what he should have done differently, both years ago and today, but that wouldn't help them now. "You know I'm not implying we give up, Gabriella."

He sat back on the floor and joined her in eating a granola bar. He huffed. "I had hoped to take you to dinner tonight to catch up." He held up the stale bar of oats. "Not exactly what I had in mind."

Gabriella put a hand on her chest. "You wanted to go to dinner?"

He couldn't read if she was just surprised or concerned. "Yeah, we used to be good friends. I regret not staying in touch."

Her shoulders dropped, as if relieved. Luke wished she looked more eager. He needed to focus on the here and now before he embarrassed himself. "Let's put our heads together. We've been avoiding the obvious—who might notice we're missing? Anyone expecting to hear from you or meet you tonight?" He steeled himself for the answer.

Her eyes turned downcast. "No. I wish. I've only been in town since the funeral. My friends and I were going to get together Sunday night. I don't think we can last two more days in here." Her eyes drifted to the ceiling. "Well, we could, but my aunt—" She inhaled sharply.

Luke recognized the signs of shock. She was going to crumble if he didn't help keep her focused. "No one else would be trying to call you? Get in touch? No appointments or...uh...boyfriend?" The question slipped out before he could stop himself. Luke grabbed another granola bar. Who was stress eating now?

"No. Sad, right? I'm a strong introvert, you know."

He grinned. "I remember. It always struck me funny how you knew you wanted to teach—standing in front of all those students—yet hated to go out to big events."

She shrugged. "It's the introvert's way. Teaching or speaking is totally different than interacting with other people...especially strangers." She broke off another hunk of the granola bar with her fingers. "What about you? An extrovert like yourself should have lots of people expecting you."

He could see the anticipation in her eyes. He raised an eyebrow, not expecting she'd volley the question back at him. Too bad his answer would only disappoint her. "I had a chili cook-off at the church I planned to attend, but no one is going to blink if I don't show up."

She leaned forward, her mouth parted, her eyes wide. "What about your receptionist? Won't she expect you to check back in?"

He groaned. "She's a temp. So no, I told her to leave as soon as she was done...as I imagine she did quite a while ago."

"Drives me crazy we don't have any way to judge what time it is." Gabriella jumped up to standing and paced back and forth. "I wish he'd stop drilling. I can't think straight knowing he's so determined." She halted her step. "No girlfriend?"

He fought to keep a smile off his face. "No."

She shrugged nonchalantly. "Have you, uh…dated since you and *Rose* broke up?" She scrunched up her nose. "I'm sorry. I don't know why I said her name like that."

"Because she hurt you," he said. Rose had stolen her fiancé, and it's what Gabriella would remember every time she set her eyes on Luke. He should've known.

"And *you*."

"Yes, but it's been a long time. It stung a lot, but it doesn't bother me anymore. I'm pretty sure they got married and divorced soon after."

"Cheaters never win," she muttered.

He raised an eyebrow. "But I think Thad remarried soon after."

She cocked her head and shook her hand in the air. "I don't care. I wouldn't be interested in him anyway. I'm just thankful I saw his true colors before I sent out wedding invitations."

Luke hated how relieved that little statement made him feel.

Gabriella resumed her pacing. "What about your family? You have like a ton of brothers, right?"

Luke gulped. For a split second, he thought she was thinking about marrying one of his brothers. Why did women change subjects so fast? She no doubt was referring to who would notice he was missing. "Yeah, but none of them live around here. They're all in California and Oregon. I've been trying to talk Matt into moving here once he's done with school."

He held out his palms. He could tell he'd disappointed her. "I'm afraid no one is going to be looking for me." The words hit him in the gut. It was true. No one would notice. In college he'd been all about developing close friendships, but ever since he started his own business, he felt he had something to prove. Work was his highest priority.

Home was his office. He slept in whatever furnished, model home was most current in order to be close to the subdivision process. He needed to make sure they stayed on schedule and supervise the foreman, which triggered a memory. "Believe it or not, my brother David and my sister-in-law, Aria, faced the mafia last year. The Russian mafia, in fact." He shook his head. "Wish we could call him now."

Gabriella's mouth dropped. "How'd they fare?"

He almost bragged on his brother's ingenuity but didn't want to rub in the fact that David was so resourceful, while Luke sat stuck in a safe room with no ideas. "They were saved by the authorities, eventually." He leveled a heavy gaze on her.

She rolled her eyes. "If my aunt Freddie's life wasn't in danger this wouldn't be an argument. I'd gladly risk my own reputation, but I'm not risking her life."

"What do you mean your reputation?"

She picked up the diary and flipped through the pages with an angry carelessness. "Apparently the Mirabella family sent in a so-called anonymous donation that can be easily traced back to them. They thought they needed an added threat to discredit my nonprofit to keep them in line." She held up a finger. "See? That just proves they have the wrong family. If they knew my mother at all, they'd have known that she wouldn't have given a threat like that the time of day and neither would I."

She shivered. A chill ran up Luke's spine as well. "It's getting cold in here," she whispered.

Luke strained his ears. The drilling had stopped a moment ago. "He's trying to freeze us out." He grabbed the red velour throw out of the storage container and draped it across her shoulders. She looked up and smiled. Her eyes and whole face lit the room when she smiled, and he was struck with a desire to kiss her. The mere thought jolted him upright.

He reached for the vent on the ground next to the dresser and slid the lever so it would close. Air still hissed through the closed slats. "And if we weren't in a closet full of blankets and dry clothes Rodrigo might've succeeded." He frowned. "You know what I don't get? What if there was a fire? Wouldn't your mom have wanted another exit?"

She pointed upward. Nothing remained on the shelving unit above Gabriella's head except a bright red fire extinguisher. "And there's a fire safety ladder underneath my bed," she said. "Besides, I don't think fire could get through these walls."

"It's not flames I'm worried about, it's the smoke." He rose on his tiptoes to see above the shelf. "I thought I saw a vent up there. Did your mom opt for the separate ventilation system?"

She threw up her hands. "I wish I knew. Your guess is as good as mine."

Luke tried to imagine how he'd feel in her position. The grief alone would probably be his undoing. He couldn't fathom wrestling with an alternate identity. Putting himself in her shoes only increased the frustration instead of prompting ideas to help.

Trapped. Caged. The words floated through his mind. He closed his eyes to calm and pictured an open field and exhaled slowly until his heart slowed slightly. Staying busy seemed the best option for the moment. "If you don't know, let's find out. If Rodrigo's smart enough to try to freeze us out, he might be smart enough to try to gas us out through the air ducts."

Her eyes widened. "With what?"

"I don't know." He should've kept his big mouth closed. He wondered what kind of chemicals might be on the property and whether the furnace operated off natural gas or electricity, but Gabriella didn't need another thing to worry about. "I'm sure we're fine. The developer in me just wants to know how she set up the room. It may give me an idea on how to get out."

He grabbed the bottom dresser drawer and flipped it over, dumping out the contents. "I just need a little boost." He stepped on it but his fingers only grazed the wall past the shelf. He stepped down to find Gabriella had already flipped over another drawer to stack.

"It won't be steady," she said. "I'll try to spot you."

He laughed. "I don't recommend that. If I fell on you, you'd snap in two."

Her dark eyes flashed. "I'm made of tougher stuff than that." He tried not to smile as she repeated the same words he'd said in the lake. She stood out of the way, though.

This time, he could reach the vent, where a separate system could be attached. His hands felt no air rushing through it. Maybe he needed to activate it, and that would shut down the main one? If only he could ask his brother David. Luke pulled on the grate and it easily slipped out. "Flashlight, please?"

She slipped the cold metal into his outstretched hand. He flicked the flashlight on and aimed it inside the vent. It stretched about sixteen inches until another metal sheet closed it off. Great. "She didn't opt for the extra system."

"Well, if she made this place for burglars she probably didn't think they'd be smart enough to mess with gassing us out."

The beam did catch something though. Stacks of paper? His jaw dropped. Money? He reached for it, his nails catching the paper straps that held the piles together.

Shifting on his tiptoes, he grasped it…and the dresser drawer below his feet shifted. The flashlight and the cash flew out of his hands. He grasped the top of the shelf but his fingertips didn't hold. He dropped. His thigh hit the edge of the drawer. A howl escaped him as he rolled off and squeezed the area around his wound.

"Are you okay?"

He nodded, despite the fire spreading up his hip. Had he ripped his wound back open? Cash floated down like confetti all around him. He gritted his teeth and the pain lessened to a throbbing. No moisture, so maybe the Steri-Strips managed to hold. He lifted his left hand, palm out, and a hundred-dollar bill floated to a rest. Assuming they were all Benjamin Franklins, there had to be upward of thirty thousand dollars in cash in the room.

Gabriella's face paled. "It's true, then." Her head dropped into her hands. "My mom was in the mafia."

SEVEN

The drilling noise ceased. She slid her hands down until she peeked over her fingertips. "It stopped." The sudden quiet in the room served as a jolt of clarity. Gabriella dropped her hands. She couldn't afford to stop and cry. She needed to think straight.

Luke stood up and pulled her into a hug. The warmth and strength from his arms and chest softened a hardened part of her heart. Gabriella couldn't remember the last time she'd been held, been comforted in such a way. She wanted to grab on and never let go. Her throat ached with a held-back sob. If she gave in to his comfort, she'd lose it and the tears would flow. Once that dam broke she knew it would take time she didn't have to get herself back together. She couldn't let her guard down now. She straightened and hardened her features.

Luke stepped back, but his fingers lingered on her shoulders. "I'm so sorry you have to deal with this... and with me in your face to boot."

"What do you mean? I told you I'm glad I'm not in this alone." She searched his eyes. In the dim lighting they looked royal blue.

"I know. But me specifically here reminding you about Thad with so much to deal with..."

That name, even when referring to another person, always made her flinch. She scrunched up her face. "Why are you talking about Thad? Thad is the farthest thing from my mind. I... I've been over him for years." She took a small breath. "Oh. Is it because you're thinking about *Rose*?"

She'd done it again. Why couldn't she say her name without sounding like a jealous girlfriend? "I remind you of what you lost with her."

His lips turned downward in an exaggerated fashion. "No. I thought you were the one having a problem. The breakup didn't hit me as hard as you."

Why did guys have to act all macho? Why did he have to make it a comparison? Did he mean to imply her heart got stomped on the hardest?

She narrowed her eyes. "As I said before, I'm fine. Thad-wise. So you can stop bringing it up. I'm not fine about this situation or my mom lying to me." She threw a hand up toward his chest, and he dropped his arms. "At least you'll *eventually* have someone looking for you. You still have family." She pointed her fingers to her heart. "If I lose my aunt, I've got no one. They were my only fam—" Her voice cracked as the lights disappeared. The small beam from the flashlight remained.

It flickered and went black.

Her senses heightened, and she reached her hands out, widening her eyes. Blackness permeated every direction she looked. The room didn't lighten. Her vision never adapted because there were no light sources to adapt to in the room.

Fingers brushed against hers.

"Gabriella?"

"Yes." She grabbed onto his fingers. "I think when you fell, your scream gave Rodrigo ideas. He wants to scare us now."

He scoffed. "I *didn't* scream. It was more of a manly wail."

"Luke?" Her heart pounded. Her eyes burned from the lack of blinking. She wanted—needed—to see something, anything. "I'm scared. I admit it. I feel like a big baby, but I hate the dark. I hate feeling trapped." Her words came out so fast and hurried she forgot to breathe. Her head spun, and she panted, attempting to fight off the dizzy feeling.

"Gabriella. It's okay. I'm here." He spoke in a low voice, just barely above a whisper. He pulled her fingers toward him and wrapped her in a hug. "Just breathe." His chin rested on top of her head.

The closeness gave her the courage to close her eyes. Nothing remained but his heartbeat, steady. Her own heart slowed. The dizzy feeling passed, but exhaustion swooped in and took its place.

She wanted to sleep, wanted to forget. "I'm sorry," she whispered. "I'm embarrassed I fell apart like that."

"You don't need to explain." His words vibrated through his chest. "Everyone has fears."

She straightened and grabbed his forearms just in case her head decided to spin again. "Is that so? I can't imagine Luke McGuire having any fear."

The silence seemed to echo in the steel room.

"Horses," he finally said.

She guffawed. She didn't mean to, but it couldn't be helped. The picture of big, strong Luke afraid of such beautiful creatures didn't compute. "Sorry. I didn't mean to laugh." She cleared her throat to keep the humorous image at bay. "Horses," she repeated, her inflection revealing her disbelief.

He grabbed her hand and lifted it until her fingertips brushed against his hair. Her heart beat wildly at the intimate gesture.

"I have a scar here."

Her fingers sank into his hair and felt a raised area. He dropped his hand away from hers, but Gabriella followed the line along his scalp. It traveled for what seemed like a good six inches. She pulled back. "What happened?"

"My grandpa had horses. I was helping him clean the stable while my brother brushed the horse. It was going to be my turn to take a ride that day, but something spooked the horse and—"

She gasped, visualizing horse hooves. "It kicked you?"

"In the head. Had to have surgery and a stent placed to keep down the swelling for several months."

She couldn't imagine how hard that must have been. "How old were you?"

"Six."

Her face heated. A small boy against a horse's powerful kick turned her stomach. "It's amazing you lived to tell the tale."

"Yes. As my mom likes to remind me of repeatedly."

She should've known better than to judge his fears so hastily. "I'd be scared of them too, if I were you. How horrible."

"It's in the past. I stay away from them and do just fine."

"Then it's good I didn't take you to the stables."

He remained silent for a few seconds. "There are still horses on the property?"

"Two of them."

"I…uh…assumed you'd sold them before you came to me."

"I haven't had time, but that's the plan. I put feelers out a couple days ago. It shouldn't take long to find them new digs. They're pretty mild-mannered and mostly graze in the pasture, but someone does have to check up on them every couple of days."

She heard him shift next to her. "Did I see batteries in the storage box?"

She mentally pictured the container. "I think so, but they looked corroded to me. Maybe there's just a short in the flashlight bulb."

"If it uses LED bulbs, we should be in business."

Gabriella didn't want to get her hopes up. "Did you taste the granola bars? I'm sure Mom didn't frequently replenish the emergency box. The flashlight is probably ancient."

The space beside her suddenly seemed void. He'd moved from his spot. Her heart went back into overdrive. She wanted to bang on the doors or take her chances and unlock the dead bolts and run. But that was what Rodrigo wanted. She didn't want to admit it to Luke in the lake, but he'd likely been right—Rodrigo didn't care if Luke lived, but he wanted her alive until he got what he wanted.

The screeching of metal against metal made her want to scream. "What are you doing?"

"Sorry. Twisting open the flashlight. Checking the batteries as best I can. Sometimes there is a short in the connection."

The screeching returned, followed by a couple of thumps and then, mercifully, a small beam of light. "We probably should touch it the least amount as possible so it won't go out again."

The shadows emphasized the lines in his face, particularly his lips. He set the flashlight on its end and leaned back onto his hands. "We need to take advantage of the light while we have it. Devour that diary and see if you can come up with anything to help us. Anything at all."

She fingered the leather book. "I don't think Mom wrote in it very often. Didn't seem to be much new."

He shrugged. "You might read it with new insight now, though." He leaned forward and placed a hand on her forearm. "I know it's going to be hard."

Even in the dark he could see right through her. She was making excuses because she didn't know if she could handle reading any more of her mother's words. The pain of losing Mom, coupled with the betrayal of finding about her other life, squeezed her throat until it hurt. She wanted to do anything but read Mom's thoughts and feelings right now. "It's so unlikely it'll help," she whispered.

He nodded. "I know. And yet, here we are."

Gabriella tilted her head to the left and to the right, trying to ease the knots forming between her shoulder blades. "You're right."

She held the book up to the weak light and began reading. The first words seemed familiar. As a child, she'd snuck into her mother's room countless times to peek in the journal. It beckoned her, especially when she could tell her mom and great-aunt had been fighting or when she suspected one of the contractors had a crush on Mom.

The journal always disappointed, though. Bible verses and things she was thankful for filled most of the pages.

Luke made it hard for her to concentrate. He rifled through the dressers again and pulled out another fleece throw. Luke stepped over the storage container and offered it to her. "The temperature keeps dropping. You need to stay warm."

Now that he said it, she realized the temperature had dipped further. The chill hadn't registered as a possible reason why her muscles wouldn't relax. She accepted and wrapped the throw around herself in such a way that she could lean against the wall while she read. "I'd say this was more of a thankfulness journal than a diary."

Luke pulled out the box of chocolates again, this time sampling one before offering her the box. "These kept better than the granola bars." He jutted his chin toward the journal. "Not a bad idea. My mom always told me that joy was something on the outside expressed by faith on the inside. She said the key was focusing on whatever was true, noble, right, pure, admirable—"

"You're paraphrasing another verse in Philippians."

"—lovely…"

His eyes looked straight into hers when he said the last word, warming her from head to toe. She dropped her gaze back to her mother's writing and wondered if her hair had steamed dry. The thought brought a smile to her face. "You better put those away," she said, referring to the chocolate box. "We can't run for our lives if we have a stomachache."

"See?" He grinned. "That's hopeful talk."

* * *

Luke jabbed a thumb over his shoulder. "Rodrigo's only been drilling on the door that leads to your mother's room. What if we slipped out the door that goes into your room?"

"Do you remember what that door felt like? It's a beast to unlock and move. There's no quick in and out."

Luke placed his hands on his hips. "So we do our best. And, if we don't succeed, and he catches us, we offer him the cash."

Her head darted around. "Where is it?"

Luke lifted a drawstring bag from behind the storage container. "I gathered it while you were reading." He handed it to her. "Roughly thirty-five thousand dollars."

"You counted it?"

He hoped the darkness worked in his favor as his face flushed. The allure of money had always been strong and something he battled. He knew he could only serve one master and had decided long ago the Lord would always win, but there was something about stacks of cash…and he knew someone as sweet and giving as Gabriella would never understand that. "It made sense to count while I picked it up."

She kept her head down but lifted her eyes. "You think he might take it and leave?"

Luke wanted to say yes, but in his heart he knew. "No. At most it'll be a distraction. Although, I pray I'm wrong, and he leaves."

Gabriella nodded.

"So we're in agreement? We try to make a run for it?"

"Doesn't it make more sense to wait until he starts drilling again?"

Luke shook his head. "No, that'd make him closer."

"But the noise of the drill would actually work in our favor as we open the opposite door. Besides, we won't know where he is if he's not drilling."

"Fair point, but then we'd have to walk down the hallway to get to the stairs. He'd see us. There's no way we could avoid him then."

She reached for his hands, her eyes wide. "Remember? There's a fire safety ladder underneath my bed. If we timed it right and were quiet, we could go out the window." Her eyes drifted down. "Your leg. It wouldn't be easy."

The mere mention made his wound throb, but he couldn't let that stop the means to her safety. "You don't worry about that. My arms can do most of the work."

She smirked. "Good at the monkey bars, were you?"

"I don't know about that, but my dad often told me and my brothers to stop monkeying around." He stepped closer to their possible escape. "So we're agreed. He starts drilling and we—"

"Go to the barn," she finished.

"Go to the police," he said simultaneously.

She growled. "I already told you I can't do that." She sighed. "But you can. If we make it out of here, go. Get to safety. Tell the police there's been a break-in at my place, but please don't mention me. I at least need a chance to try to save my aunt."

He could not believe this woman. As if he could leave her alone. He shrugged but didn't agree.

She stood and grabbed the fire extinguisher off the top shelf. He gestured toward her. "What do you plan on doing with that?"

Her eyes flashed. "I don't know, but I feel safer holding something. Have any better ideas?"

As if on cue, the high-pitched hum started up again. Rodrigo had resumed drilling. Luke crossed to the opposite door. "As a matter of fact, I do. I'll open the door the least amount as possible. I'll slip out while you stay inside. Once I get the ladder attached to the window, I'll motion for you to come out and go out the ladder first."

"But—"

"I'm not budging," Luke said firmly. It was his harebrained idea, for lack of a better one, and he wouldn't live with himself if he put her in harm's way.

She exhaled and joined him at the door. "Fine."

"You'll stay here until I give the all clear, and if Rodrigo enters the room you'll shut the door back up."

Her eyes widened. "I am not leaving you out there with him!"

"You will, or we're not even trying this."

She pursed her lips.

"We have a deal?"

She shrugged. He knew that trick. "Gabriella?"

Her eyes flicked his way. "I may not agree with you, but I heard you. I'll try to do what you're asking. It's the best I can do for now."

Luke stared into her beautiful eyes. "I don't like it, but I suppose I'll take it." He placed his hand on the top bolt. "Ready?"

She nodded.

Luke strained his ear, focusing on the drilling, and clicked the three bolts. He paused and listened. The drilling continued. Rodrigo had apparently gotten the hang of the slow and steady process that prevented the drill bit from breaking. He looked over at Gabriella. She gripped the fire extinguisher so tight it was almost comical. What did she hope to accomplish with that?

Gabriella nodded, and Luke pulled on the door.

It opened with a pop. The noise caused every muscle in Luke's body to tense. The drilling stopped. Gabriella moved one hand to the door as if ready to slam it closed again.

The high-pitched squeal cued up. Luke exhaled. He pulled the door further into the safe room until there was barely enough space for him to slip out. "Stay here," he whispered.

Luke shimmied his way into the light purple bedroom. The change in lighting surprised him. The sun had almost completed its descent. The dim light made the room seem darker, and the shadows from furniture and lamps set his teeth on edge. Laminate wood flooring covered the room. He hadn't expected that.

His still-damp dress shoes made a slight squeak as he stepped forward. Great. He looked over his shoulder to find Gabriella peeking her head out of the safe room with a finger over her lips. As if he could control what sounds the soles of his shoes made.

She pointed frantically to the left side of the bed. Ah. That's where he should start looking for the fire ladder, if it was still there. When was the last time she'd checked the location? What if her mom had moved it?

He sank down onto his knees and peeked. Nothing appeared underneath the bed except dust bunnies and a square shadow toward the head of the bed. He reached out, and as soon as his fingers clutched metal, he knew he'd found it.

Luke pulled the ladder toward him. The sound of metal scratching on wood caused him to stop as soon as he started. He strained his ears. The drilling continued. He would just need to get it over with. He yanked and the metal hooks slid to the edge of the bed. He hopped up on his knees and gathered the rope, slats and metal supports in his arms.

He turned and almost hollered as Gabriella stood two inches from his face. "I told you to stay put," he whispered.

"You need help," she hissed back. "I'll hold this while you open the window. It'll be faster." She set the fire extinguisher down on the wood floor at the foot of the bed.

Gabriella didn't see him roll his eyes as he acquiesced and handed her the tightly compressed fire ladder. Her knees buckled slightly, and she wore a pinched expression. He should've warned her it wasn't lightweight, close to thirty or forty pounds.

Even with a different perspective he couldn't see clear enough to figure out how to unlatch the ropes. For that, he'd need to get it closer to the window.

Luke flicked the lock between the two window frames and shoved the glass upward. He almost groaned aloud. It hadn't occurred to him that there'd be a screen. Okay, maybe it was good she came to help. Every second counted.

He grabbed and pulled on the black tabs located on either side of the screen frame. The frame slipped out of the track. He wrestled with it, trying to turn it diagonally to bring it fully inside the house.

"Luke," she whispered. "We have to go now."

"Almost there," he muttered. The background noise stopped unless he counted the birds cawing, the crickets singing and the toads croaking. He hadn't anticipated the sounds that would waft in through the open window. A breeze carried the telltale smell of sulfur from the forest fires in the west. The drilling had stopped. Maybe Rodrigo had sensed the breeze? Maybe he wanted a small break before starting up again?

Footsteps in the hallway. Luke stiffened. They were so close to escaping. Maybe Rodrigo needed something from downstairs. Another footstep. They couldn't risk another second.

He tossed the screen onto the mattress. "Get back into the—"

The tip of a gun peeked around the hallway door to the room. It was too late.

EIGHT

Gabriella spun around to face the darkened doorway as Rodrigo stepped into the room, a smirk on his face. "Well, what do we have—"

Instinct propelled her arms up and out, shoving the heavy bundle of metal and rope into the air. The ladder soared directly toward Rodrigo.

"Catch," she yelled.

If there was one thing she'd learned from being a public school teacher, it was that distraction could be her ally. The shadows in the room worked to her advantage as Rodrigo's expression morphed into surprise and confusion. He flinched and opened his arms wide to catch it. The rubber ends on the tips of the metal hooks slammed into Rodrigo's chest. He howled as the ladder unlatched itself against him.

Crack! The gun fired into the ceiling as the metal and ropes bounced off his chest and onto the wooden floor.

She bent down and grabbed the fire extinguisher she'd set down on the ground at the foot of the bed. The weight of the metal container always surprised her. How could foam weigh so much?

"What are you doing? Go, go, go," Luke shouted. His arm snaked around her waist and pulled her up and along with him, as if he were a quarterback and she was a football on the way to a touchdown. Her toes dragged against the floor, but she kept her eyes firmly focused on Rodrigo.

Gabriella yanked the pin from the fire extinguisher and depressed the trigger as Luke carried her the few feet to the barely open safe-room door. The white foam sprayed across the room as she twisted the nozzle from side to side.

The goo slapped her target right across his face. She didn't ease up and moved her aim to Rodrigo's hand, hoping she could spray the gun right out or at least make it hard to hold.

Rodrigo kicked the ladder across the room and wiped away the foam with his forearm in one swift motion. He roared with rage.

The ladder slid and hit Luke in the foot. He released Gabriella's waist and shoved her behind the steel door, stepping directly beside her as they both slipped inside the safe room.

She stepped to the side as a gunshot rang out. Something flew through her hair, mere inches from her hairline, and dinged into the wall behind her. Had she been hit and just wasn't feeling it yet?

She kicked the edge of the door. "Close it, close it, close it," she chanted.

Luke barreled all of his body weight against the safe-room door. While it only had a foot to go, the door closed at a snail's pace as Rodrigo sprinted, full force, toward them.

Rodrigo reached out his gun again. This time he

didn't seem to care whether or not she lived as he aimed at the spot between her eyes.

Gabriella lifted up the heavy fire extinguisher over her head and threw it full force through the eight-inch gap. The round end of the bottom of the can bounced off Rodrigo's forehead as Luke threw his body weight against the steel door until it slammed shut. Gabriella dropped to her knees and twisted the bottom bolt shut as Luke worked on the top and the center.

Dull pings slammed into the door. Bulges only inches away from her eyes formed and worked their way up the door. Her breath ragged, she scooted backward. Her heart attempted to jump out of her throat as she wrestled against the sudden nausea. They could've been killed.

Luke spun toward her as she accidentally bumped the standing flashlight in the middle of the room. The light flickered but remained lit.

"How many bullets did your mom have?" he asked.

"Quite a stockpile," she admitted. More bulges in the door appeared. The impacts didn't quit until Rodrigo must have released another clip of bullets. Bumps covered the entire inside of the door. "Someone's got an anger problem."

Luke's eyes widened as he stared at her. He guffawed as he shook his head. "Well, I would, too, if I was at the other end of your self-defense tactics." He sat down beside her. "You're something else, Gabriella."

She studied him and replayed his words. "I can't tell if that's a positive or negative in your view."

He laughed the nervous laugh of someone in shock. "You're unique, one of a kind."

"Again, you're not being clear." She couldn't help the smile spreading across her face.

He faced her and took her hand, sending invisible sparks shooting up her spine. "You no doubt saved my life." His eyes narrowed. "While I'm upset you put yourself in harm's way, I can't dismiss that I wouldn't have breath left in my body if you hadn't done what you did." His eyes bulged. "Catch? You said catch?" He slapped the carpet beside him, laughing. "That'll teach him to mess with a teacher."

She shrugged, trying not to be bothered that he'd dropped her hand. How could someone's touch both bring comfort and a thrill at the same time?

Gabriella reached up and touched the side of her head, feeling for any sign of wetness. Her fingertips combed through her hair and swiped along her scalp.

"What are you doing?"

"Just making sure I didn't get grazed. I'd have thought I would've felt it, but I've also heard about shock…" Her fingers touched something rough. As if a few strands of hair had been singed directly above her ear. She pulled the remaining strands forward, in hopes she could take a look.

"I thought I heard a gunshot, but I didn't realize the bullet made its way in." Luke leaned forward and touched her hair. "That was too close, Gabriella. I'm glad we don't have matching scars…or worse." His eyes drifted from her hair to her face, then to her lips.

Her mouth went dry. "Me, too." The intense look in his eyes scared her almost as much as the thought of getting shot. She'd never forget the moment he'd almost kissed her.

It had happened years ago—a couple of months after they'd learned about their fiancés' betrayal. They spent a lot of time together, because frankly no one else understood their pain and it turned out their personalities complemented each other nicely.

They became best friends within weeks. And when Luke tried to make it something more, it terrified her. She'd turned him away, worried they were diving into a rebound relationship that would only hurt the friendship.

Her cheeks heated at the memory. Gabriella didn't want a repeat of the last time. Even now, he seemed to make light of the fact his fiancée cheated on him. As if his heart had never been fully invested, as if he wasn't devastated.

She couldn't give her heart to someone who wasn't going to take it seriously. If his heart wasn't all in for his own fiancée, she didn't want to risk opening herself up to loving someone more than they would ever love her.

And if she thought she wasn't ready for a relationship back then, she certainly wasn't ready for one now. She didn't even know who she was anymore. Gabriella needed to do something, say something, before he moved any closer.

"Rodrigo made it personal," Gabriella said, attempting a half smile. She flipped her hair back over her shoulder. "He ruined my hairstyle."

The glib comment worked. Luke snickered and looked away.

His eyes widened, and his mouth went slack. He shifted out of his sitting position and crossed the room. His fingers brushed over the wall directly next to her mom's side of the closet. She squinted to see the tiny indention, the source of his study.

"This bullet barely missed you." His voice raw, he dropped his head in his hand. He shook his head. "I'm sorry, Gabriella. It was a horrible idea."

"No. No it wasn't. We almost made it." She replayed the past few minutes in her mind. There were about a million things she would've done differently if she had to do it again, first being that she would've gone with him in the very beginning to speed things along instead of waiting.

"It put you in danger. If something had happened to you…"

Her face heated as she digested his words. They really had cheated death. The very thought reminded her that her aunt still remained in harm's way with Benito. How was she supposed to save her aunt's life if she couldn't get free of Rodrigo?

"Hey."

She looked up at Luke's greeting. He smiled softly. "Don't go there."

Gabriella locked eyes with him, and a shiver ran up her spine. "How'd you know where my mind was going?"

He shrugged. "It's only natural." He pointed at the diary she'd foolishly cast aside. What if their escape plan had worked, but she'd left the book behind? "Let's focus on what we *can* do. How about you keep reading the journal?"

She took a shaky breath and flipped it open. Just like her mother's favorite verse, Luke reminded her that she needed to take her thoughts captive and focus on whatever was good…or in this case, the only positive thing she could accomplish while trapped in a giant steel box.

Luke walked around the perimeter of the small space. It seemed more like a dungeon to him. Her mom had built it almost thirty years ago. Too bad she hadn't kept up with the upgrades. Right now, LED interior lighting would've helped him out. But even three decades ago, the manufacturers would have made an extra door that could only be accessed from the inside. He was sure of it.

"And you can't remember your mom ever telling you about an extra exit? Not even in emergencies?"

Gabriella closed her eyes and shook her head. "If she had, I'm sure I would've used it to sneak out at night."

"Excuse me?" Luke put two hands on his hips.

She laughed at his reaction. "I went through a rebellious phase. For a while there, Mom and Aunt Freddie took the fire ladder from my room because they couldn't trust me."

"Where would you go? You'd sneak out and meet boys?"

"Nah. I never went that far." She twisted her mouth diagonally. "I did let my friends in through the gate sometimes, though, so we could swim in the lake in the middle of the night."

He frowned. "I thought it was electronic."

She nodded. "I know how to open it manually at the box." She sighed. "There was one time I simply walked down the street to the general store to get candy."

Luke tried to picture the closest store. There was nothing for miles. "That's a long walk."

She sighed. "Almost five miles. Mom was out of chocolates, and my craving couldn't be squelched." She laughed. "At the time I remember thinking I was invincible. That I could outrun and outwit anything that came my way. It terrified my mom. But I eventually wised up." She scrunched her nose in disgust, seemingly at her own reference to wise guys.

"Was there something specific that opened your eyes?"

Gabriella shrugged. "The real world. Friends had bad experiences, and I took them to heart." She blinked and shook her head. "But…but I do have some vague memory that there wasn't always carpet in here." She stroked the fibers underneath her fingertips.

Luke's heart sped up. "Really? When do you think that changed?"

"I don't remember, and I'm not positive so don't get your hopes up."

His optimism refused to be tamed, spinning out of control. He could do something useful. "I think I better start pulling up the carpet." He pointed at her. "You keep reading. This could take a while without any tools at my disposal."

She squinted. "I wish we had more light. My eyes are having a hard time adjusting to the changing shadows. Especially while you're moving around."

Luke moved to the far end of the room where he'd disturb the light source the least. He kicked off his soggy shoes. He'd be able to get more traction without the damp things on his feet, and hopefully they'd dry faster if he turned them over on top of the vent. Now that the adrenaline had worked its way out of his system, the chill began to seep into his bones.

Gabriella grabbed a blanket and wrapped it around her shoulders. She opened the book across her lap. "Not a single one of my mom's entries go by without the words: *I am so thankful for my Gab—Gabriella.*" Her head dropped as her voice broke. Luke wanted to comfort her, to pull her in close, but she pulled her knees up and placed one arm around her legs as if in her own fort.

She needed space.

Luke moved to an edge of the flooring and grabbed the fibers of the carpet and pulled. His muscles strained and…nothing.

He leaned back on his heels to think it through. The floor underneath the carpet was likely steel. In that case, the installation team wouldn't have used tacks to lay down the carpet. They would've used glue.

Great. He needed to go up against industrial-strength glue without any tools. He sighed. His dad or brother, the resourceful construction experts, would've known what to do. They always did. Luke was more a businessman than a builder.

He exhaled and closed his eyes. If he had an exit door in the floor but had a headstrong daughter that he wanted to keep it a secret from, what would he do?

Luke grinned. If it had been him, he'd glue the carpet down heavily everywhere…except closest to where the door would be. That way it'd be unlikely the teenager would ever find out. And over the spot with the exit, he would either only lightly glue it or not at all. He dared to hope that Gabriella's mom would follow the same thought pattern.

He moved to the closest corner and squatted. He dug his fingers into the carpet fibers on either side of the sharp corner. He inhaled and pulled, pressing into his heels and throwing his shoulders backward as he harnessed the power in his legs. The carpet gave, a ripping sound echoing off the walls, but it coincided with the stinging yank on his wound. He fell back and exhaled. His leg throbbed.

Now the question was whether the carpet corner had been lightly glued or if he just had a better vantage point this time around, with proper motivation. Either way, it looked to be a long night. And his wound wasn't going to take much more of that.

The high-pitched whir started up again. Great. Rodrigo had gone back to drilling.

He examined the dimly lit room. The other corners would require some rearrangement of furniture and boxes, not to mention disrupt Gabriella. Her body shook slightly, her head dipped close to the pages of the book, but if she was crying it wasn't audible. It pained him to watch her sorrow without any comfort to bring, without any solutions to offer. So he turned back to try again.

He grabbed the carpet and pulled again. It gave another six inches.

Luke peeked underneath the flap he'd pulled. Yep, steel. After five more pulls with very little result, he decided to move around some furniture. He moved the dresser into the bathroom. His knuckles scraped along the door frame as he pressed, not caring about the tight fit. He'd push harder, enough to make it work. He needed room to maneuver the carpet more.

The now-empty corner gave the same result. It gave very slightly and wreaked havoc on his leg. He quickly rebandaged the wound in the bathroom. When he reentered to try again, Gabriella's head hung low. Her shoulders rose and fell in steady movement. How anyone could fall asleep to the whir of the drill was beyond him, but by now it had to be late into the night. And after the stress of the day and no immediate hope of a getaway or rescue, the escape of sleep enticed him, as well.

Her head nodded and the diary dropped from her fingertips to the floor. It fell open to the middle. Luke remained standing and stared at the pages for a moment. Twice he'd encouraged her to read it, and twice she'd shut down.

His leg throbbed to the rhythm of the drill's grinding outside the door. If he took a short break, he could read the diary for her. An impartial party might be able to see any clues she'd left for her daughter. Or the authorities.

His mind made up, Luke grabbed another blanket, got as comfortable as possible with his leg killing him, and began to read.

Freedom's been on my mind a lot. We lived so much of our life in bondage that when I got physical freedom I thought that would be enough. But after I found freedom in Christ, I realized just how much Freddie and I had been missing out. I pray Gabriella never has to experience such bondage. It seems the time is near to give it all up. I've long stopped looking over my shoulder in fear, but I hope as I pray for the right timing, that I don't open up the door to danger.

NINE

"Gabriella..." She felt jostled as she fought against her heavy eyelids.

"What?" She blinked rapidly. The left side of her neck ached as if it'd been twisted in a vise. Her hand flew back and pressed into the flesh to ease the pain.

"You fell asleep." Luke's scratchy voice jolted her.

"I did? How long?" She sat upright and blinked, praying it'd been a nightmare. She looked around the room—their prison—and wished she could go back to sleep. Her dreams had to be more pleasant than the nightmare she was living.

"I'm not sure. I was busy ripping up the carpet. And then I took a break—" He pressed a hand on his forehead and dragged it down to his chin. "I fell asleep, too." He slammed his back against the wall and looked upward. "I hate not having a clock."

"I know. It's maddening." Gabriella's vision adjusted. The room seemed bigger somehow. "Where's the dresser? You moved furniture?"

"Yeah, I put it in the bathroom. You were out. I rested for a moment and must have dozed off a few seconds myself. I think it's the cold. It slows down our circulation systems. We need to get moving to stay awake."

"Ironic. Rodrigo wanted to freeze us out and instead he put us to sleep." She shivered underneath the blanket and lifted her hand to her hair. While mostly dry, it remained damp closest to her scalp. "Wet hair probably didn't help. What woke you up?"

"He started drilling again when I moved the dresser out of here." He straightened and paced two steps to the left followed by two steps to the right. If he did it much longer, she'd get dizzy. "He was at it a while. I think he stopped, and that's what woke me up."

"So he might be close to breaking through? What do you think he'll do if he gets all the way through? Start shooting? Or threaten to start shooting?"

Gabriella's imagination spun into overdrive. What if the twenty-four hours were almost gone? She flung off the blanket. "Luke, I have to find out what time it is, or I'm going to go crazy. What if I slept most of the time away? How could I sleep when my great-aunt is about to die?"

Luke wrapped his arms around her. "There's no way we could've been out that long." The warmth from his embrace and words calmed her...slightly. "I think my mind kept working on it, even when I dozed off. I've been thinking," he continued, "the estate transferred quickly. So your mom must have had things in order. There was a will?"

She nodded against his shoulder and pulled away. "There were no clues if that's what you're getting at. She didn't leave me a letter or anything with even a hint—"

He held out a hand. "Humor me. What exactly did it say?"

She shrugged. "Standard legalese. It wasn't unique enough to be remembered verbatim. She left me the property, the house, the historic barn, and that's about it."

Luke frowned. "The historic barn?"

"Yeah. I don't remember it very well, but apparently we lived there years ago. I was too little to remember, and we stayed there only while the house was being built. You can't see it from the driveway or the house. It's much deeper into the property…near the stables."

"She mentioned the barn but not the stables?"

"Yeah, but it's implied—"

"The will said *historic* barn?"

Gabriella blew out a long breath, trying not to grow exasperated but failing. Maybe he needed coffee to wake up and understand her. Or maybe she wasn't making sense. "Yes, Luke, it's an old barn."

"But I need to know if you're telling me her exact wording. There isn't more than one barn on the property?"

"I don't know how I could make it any clearer."

Luke crossed his arms over his chest. "It's a clue, Gabriella. That barn isn't historic."

Energy coursed through his veins. If they were efficient, he could find the exit, get her to the police and send the authorities to the barn…all in time to save her aunt. He liked that plan.

Although, all the effort pulling up the carpet resulted in only finding more steel, and the process was the opposite of efficient, as he didn't want to disturb Gabriella while she slept.

He never intended to let her sleep so long, though,

and never dreamed he'd have fallen asleep himself. In fact, he realized now he had been dreaming about fighting to keep himself awake and searching for the exit.

"What are you talking about? The barn is a clue?" Gabriella pressed.

"There are several requirements for a building to be considered historic. Your mother would've known that."

"So?"

"The county property reports and permits indicate the barn was built in 1980. There's nothing historic about it."

"The year I was born." Gabriella put a hand on his arm. "You really think it's a clue?"

He shrugged. "I don't want to get your hopes up, but if it were me I'd start there." Hadn't he read something in the diary about wanting to show Gabriella what she'd done with the barn? Or had he dreamed it along with searching for the exit?

"Luke—" Her face scrunched up and she coughed. "Do you smell something?"

He inhaled and regretted it as his lungs, still sensitive from inhaling water, constricted. He joined her in a cough. The smell of burning moldy leaves filled the room. The small beam from the flashlight illuminated the curl of smoke soaring up to the ceiling.

Her eyes widened, and her shaky finger pointed. "Fire!"

Luke instinctively placed his hand on the steel door. The cold metal didn't help him understand the situation.

"I should've never used the fire extinguisher as a weapon," she lamented. "We have nothing."

He coughed again but ran to the other door. It also seemed cool to the touch.

"Luke, I think it might be coming from the vent."

He bent down and picked up the flashlight. The beam flickered out. "No, not now." He slapped the metal and the meager light illuminated the source of the smoke. Sure enough, smoke curled out the floor vent, up and around his shoes. "We need to get out now."

He lifted his shoes off the vent and slipped them on. "Let's go."

"No." She grabbed his arm. "That's what he wants. He's trying to smoke us out."

"Yeah, well it might work." He looked into her eyes. "Gabriella, what if the house is on fire?"

She pointed to the door. "And what if it's not, and he's waiting for us?"

Luke weighed the risk and ran to the bathroom. "Fine. Then help me." He pulled out a handful of clothes from the middle dresser. "Let's soak these and stuff them in the vents."

He turned on the bathroom faucet. Nothing. He turned to the bathtub, but it only dripped a meager stream before it dried up.

"He's turned off the water." She turned to the other room. "I think we have a couple more water bottles."

"Wait. Don't waste our only drinking water." Coughs racked his body again. He pointed the flashlight to the vent located underneath the vanity sink in the bathroom. Smoke poured through the vent, which corroborated Gabriella's theory. It seemed more likely that Rodrigo intended to smoke them out through the air ducts than that the house was on fire.

He lifted the toilet tank. At least fresh water waited there. He dunked the sweatshirt and handed it to Gabriella. "Remove the grate and stuff this in this vent."

She nodded. He took the other dry clothes, repeated the process and strode into the closet to stuff the other vent, with Gabriella on his heels. "Do you really think this will work?" she asked.

"Only temporarily."

She held a hand over her nose. "Oh, the smell. What could he be burning that stinks so bad?"

Luke pointed to the corner. "Grab your mom's diary, then help me roll up the rest of the carpet." The smell hit him as well—like moldy leaves mixed with rotting fish next to a campfire.

She coughed. "I don't think it's stopping the smoke. Do we need to add more clothes?"

Luke figured it'd been a long shot in the first place. "It's at least slowing the smoke down." He grabbed the edge of the carpet that Gabriella had been sleeping against and pulled. The crackling of the fibers ripping from the floor encouraged him. It gave so much easier than the other three corners, as if they used a different type of glue, or used less of it. Another yank and the corner pulled free.

Please help us find an exit, Lord.

Gabriella bent down, and her left hand brushed against his arm as she reached for the edge next to him. "One, two, three!"

He pulled as Gabriella threw her weight back. She slipped and fell back against the already-rolled carpet. "I guess I got a little too—" The coughs racked her body as she got on her knees.

His own chest burned. "Gabriella, this is insane. We've got no choice. We need to open the door."

"I'd rather pass out from lack of oxygen than have you get killed…and whatever else Rodrigo has planned for me." She crawled over to him. "We just need to keep our heads down low for oxygen." She frowned and stared at her right hand. "Luke…there's an odd bump."

Luke helped her stand. They both rolled the carpet up and away as fast as possible. Gabriella's foot hit something.

"Flashlight," she said.

He pointed the beam in her direction. Centered in the steel floor a small handle lay flat within an indention in the floor. She looked up, grinning.

"Don't get your hopes up. Your mom didn't opt for the separate ventilation. We don't know if this actually leads anywhere."

Her teeth flashed as her fingers wrapped around the silver handle and pulled up. Her face fell. "Maybe you're right."

Luke joined her. He twisted the upright handle to the right and something hissed. Gabriella's hands wrapped around his arm. "What was that?"

"Hydraulics? Pray, Gabriella…pray…" He stood up and pulled on the handle. It gave, and a square piece of metal similar to the thick doors swished upward, revealing…floor.

"Oh, no." Gabriella's voice sounded so distraught it almost broke him.

But he could tell instantly the flooring felt flimsy. Perhaps a combination of drywall and plywood? It'd be weak enough he could stomp through it. There was still no guarantee that Rodrigo wouldn't hear them. Luke mentally pictured what could be underneath her mother's bedroom. The garage?

"Luke." She swung the beam to the floor. The light illuminated a wooden frame just inside the steel opening. "We don't need to break it, we need to lift it." The light reflected off a loop of something silver. He reached for the thin wire and pulled. The board lifted a half inch before the wire slipped from its hold and the board smacked back down, leaving the circle of wire around his finger.

"You've got to be kidding me." How many decades had this exit gone untested?

Gabriella tried to get hold of the board with her fingernails, to no avail. "We need a knife or something." She lowered her chin to her chest and coughed again.

"Just a straight edge." What could possibly be in a closet that he could use? The beam glinted off something metallic. He hopped up and yanked the hanger off the pole and flung the dress hanging on it to the side. The hanger's hook slipped neatly through the small space, and he tugged.

The board popped up an inch before it fell back. He tried again and Gabriella's fingers darted in the space. The board fell onto her hand. "Ouch."

He threw the heavy board to the side.

"You okay?"

She cradled her hand but nodded. He made a mental note to take a look at it later. They both ducked their heads into the blackness for a deep gulp of air. Musty, dusty air, but it only irritated his lungs slightly compared to what came through the vents.

"Do you feel warmth?" he asked.

She shook her head. "No. I don't think the house is on fire."

He took the flashlight from her. The space was cavernous in length but not in height. They could easily climb down, hopefully without alerting Rodrigo. He hung his head down lower. The light washed over spiderwebs and dust bunnies the size of cats.

A raised area caught his attention. "I think we've found our exit. It's most likely the attic above the garage, but we'll need to be careful. Rodrigo will no doubt be listening for any sign of our escape."

She nodded…as the flashlight slipped from his sweaty grip and hit the bottom with a clatter.

TEN

Gabriella gaped, but she could no longer see a thing.

"I'm so sorry." Luke's voice sounded raw. "I... We have to go now or never. I'll go first."

Her eyes strained, but still she saw nothing. The sound of denim sliding along carpet and wood was followed by a soft thump. "Your turn," he whispered. "There's actually a little light from the vents at the far end."

"Mom's diary." She crawled around on her knees, feeling, searching.

"Gabriella," he called out. "We can't wait any longer."

Her throat burned as she coughed, nearing closer to the vent. He was right. He'd told her to keep the diary with her, but she'd been stubborn and wanted to help.

"Talk to me," she croaked. "I need to find the hole again."

Her heart beat wildly against her ribs. Every sensation felt foreign, and her head spun.

"I'm here," he whispered. "I'm waving my hand in the air."

"I can't see it, though." Her right index finger slipped into empty space and hit flesh. "Sorry."

"Hop down. I'll catch you."

She turned around on her belly. "Watch out. Here come my feet." She knew, logically, that it wasn't too deep. If Luke could stand at the bottom and stick his hands up, then she'd be fine, but her heart refused to believe it.

Her stomach turned—possibly from the granola bar—and her throat wanted to release a scream. Her feet dangled in air and then as she slid, strong hands gripped her waist. She gasped as he pulled, and suddenly her toes touched something solid.

"Don't move for a second. Catch your balance. We need to stay on the rafters. You're going to want to duck. The height diminishes in a second." She blinked and reached for Luke's hand. The room lightened, and she could see the boards and the odd shaping of the room. A crack in the floor a few inches behind Luke leaked the rays. "Is that why we need to stay on the two-by-fours?"

She couldn't be sure in the shadows, but it seemed like a sheepish grin. "Yes. I very nearly stepped all the way through. Good thing I have quick reflexes, or you'd have to be pulling me out of the ceiling below. I'm not used to climbing around crawl spaces anymore." He jutted his chin forward. "Hurry. In case Rodrigo heard us."

Gabriella tightened her stomach. She remembered from her workout classes that a strong core helped balance. She flung her arms out and took a step forward. But she couldn't make herself lift her back foot. Instead she shuffled, sliding her feet forward.

A series of thuds vibrated the side of the walls. "Where is that coming from?"

"I'm not sure, but it's not a good sign. If I put my hands on your shoulders, do you think you could walk faster?" His voice was soft, soothing. She knew he wanted to keep her from panicking, from thinking about Rodrigo on their trail, but it had the opposite effect.

"Yes." His firm hands on her shoulders gave her the courage to move. He wouldn't let her fall through the ceiling.

She sped to the raised box. She knelt down and flung the top off. Two feet below, the top of her mom's SUV blocked her exit. It'd be tricky to get out. The car creaked as she stepped on the top. Luke bent down and held her hand as she sat down.

"Just like recess, Gabriella. You can do it."

She squirmed until her feet slid down the window. At the last second, she ducked her head below the ceiling and slid down to the hood.

The wipers dug into her back as she turned over and slid off the car to solid ground. The windows to the side revealed the source of the light earlier. Luke grunted as he maneuvered the tight space and finally joined her. "Would the keys to this car be in here?"

"They're still upstairs in Mom's room." She pointed to the window. "You any good at reading the time based on the sun?"

Luke squinted. "Looks like the sunshine is streaming in from the east." He flashed a reassuring smile. "It's probably early morning." He lunged to the garage door and pulled a red lever down. He glanced sideways at her. "Do you have your bearings? The moment I open this door, we need to make a run for it."

They needed to get to the barn. In that scenario, they really needed to go due south, but there was the small problem of the lake in their way, plus in the event Rodrigo saw them leaving she wanted to lead him away from their true goal.

She mapped out a route in her head. He grabbed her hand and squeezed. "Gabriella, promise me that no matter what, you keep running."

He was asking her to keep going if he got shot, if Rodrigo got him. She searched his pleading eyes. She wanted to say no, to argue, to lie even, but her great-aunt was counting on her. "Okay."

Her eyes drifted to the lightweight kayak leaning vertically against the wall between the two garage doors. Her mom used to take a row every day for her exercise.

He turned to the door and in one motion swept the aluminum door straight up. "Run!"

She tossed Luke the plastic oar and grabbed the handle on the nylon deck of the kayak and tossed it over her shoulder.

His eyes widened. "What are you doing?"

"Trust me." She jogged left, around the corner toward the front of the house.

"At least let me carry that."

She ignored him and darted past their cars. If only they had keys. "Give me the oar."

He handed her the orange stick. "I hate to break it to you, but there's no way we can both fit in there." She ran until they were just underneath the willow tree branches. "We don't have to—"

"Freeze," a thick voice yelled. She peeked through the vines and saw Rodrigo from an open window on the second floor.

Crack!

A chunk of dirt six inches next to Luke flew up in the air. His eyes widened. "Duck!"

Gabriella dumped the stick in the kayak and shoved it off into the lake. She bent over, grabbed his hand and ran around the trees. She hoped, even for a split second, that it would distract or confuse Rodrigo enough to give them the chance to hide.

Another gunshot rang out as water splashed up. She sprinted until she got behind a pine tree. She pressed her hands on top of her knees and sucked in a deep breath. "You okay?"

He nodded, panting. "Yeah, let's go."

"We need to stay close to the trees." She didn't feel safe standing still any longer. She took off running and looked over her shoulder. Luke kept up, but his injured leg took more of a hop than a stride.

Ten minutes later, Gabriella slowed her pace. Her stomach rolled with the nausea that came with low blood sugar and a workout so hard she could no longer breathe. She hadn't experienced the sensation since high school track. "He can't see us from the house now."

She pointed to the row of trees. "You can't even see the lake from here. We can probably slow down a little if you need."

"I'm so turned around, Gabriella. My sense of direction is all messed up." Luke placed his hands on his lower back and puffed out his chest as he inhaled. "Let's get to the road, and then we can slow down."

She froze. "We're not headed for the road. We're going to the barn."

His eyebrows rose as his jaw hardened. "No. We're going to the police."

"Luke, we talked about this."

"Yes, and you said it was a moot point. It's not anymore, and I'm taking you to the police to get you away from this madman. They can help you and your aunt, Gabriella. You just need to give them a chance."

Her heart warmed at the concern in Luke's voice, but Benito's words replayed in her mind.

Gabriella hated the thought of them splitting up, but her eyes drifted to his leg. A slight red mark on his jeans meant the bandages weren't holding the wound. He was bleeding again. "Go," she said. "Tell them about Rodrigo, but please don't tell them about my aunt or Benito."

She held up a hand at his open mouth. "It's the best I can do. I know you've had good experiences with cops, but if my mom escaped the mafia and felt she couldn't trust law enforcement she must've had her reasons. Benito was cocky enough to leave me with a phone… and a threat with it, yes, but still. Doesn't that make you wonder if part of their confidence comes from having a mole inside the police or FBI? Or both?"

He focused on the tree line closest to the house. "Maybe, maybe not."

Gabriella could tell by his impassive face that her logic failed to work on him. She put a hand on her hip. "Besides, do you know how much time it would take to get to the police? The clock is ticking. There is no time to schedule some kind of sting before they kill my aunt."

He shook his head and raked a hand through his hair. "You win. Lead the way to the barn."

"But I told you—"

His eyes met hers. "I'm not leaving you."

"And I don't want to risk you getting shot again, and this time it'd likely be more than a graze. You saw Rodrigo. He's not going to give up until he gets me and gets what he wants."

"Then let's stop wasting time." He leaned forward, his expression determined. "I'm ready for that property tour."

Her neck tingled, and the wind carried with it the acrid scent of burning sulfur. Fire season had started early in the Northwest. Both Washington and Oregon faced severe property loss. The late spring winds and lack of rain made things worse.

"This way." She stepped past another line of trees and inhaled the scent from a blooming cherry tree in the distance. After smelling the lake water and smoke from the vents and faraway forest fires, she wanted to smell the blossoms for the rest of the day. The horrible scents seemed to be permanently burned in her senses.

Luke's stomach growled. "Too bad there's no fruit on the trees yet."

She grinned. "If we hurry, I think I can help you with that along the way."

"I had no idea how many trees you had on the land. It's like a forest."

And the one reason Gabriella felt confident Rodrigo wouldn't find them. "Mom loved the variety. She planned the land to be its own complete ecosystem."

She couldn't help the pride that puffed within at the reflection of her mom's work. If they ever got out of this alive, Luke would have to tear it all down. Her gut churned at the thought, but she needed money to take care of Aunt Freddie. All things being equal, her mom would've understood. "I'm sure you can sell the lumber for a good price before you build."

He stiffened. "What am I hearing?"

She listened to the crackling and trickling of water and understood his concern, but early mornings spent walking the land provided some of her favorite sounds. "Follow me," she whispered.

Gabriella slid through a small narrow gap in the arborvitae trees, used to help stop the wind from hitting the house and the lake.

Luke placed a hand over his wounded area and stepped past the prickly foliage to join her. She put a finger over her mouth and pointed at the swan and cygnets swimming down the bubbling creek.

"Wow." He exhaled a sound of awe. "Please tell me you don't expect me to catch and cook us a fish."

"I caught a trout with my bare hands once. True story." She almost laughed as he cringed. "No, I don't expect us to eat raw fish…or cook fish. That'd be ludicrous. If memory serves, we should have some wild raspberries to eat. They're usually untouched until the fall crop when the birds and squirrels take their fair share."

She pointed at what looked like a pond at the end of a stream surrounded by bushes and another willow tree. "If we turn left at the willow tree we could run across a few acres until we reached the barn, but we'd be in the open. No shelter. We would make for an easy target. I'm planning to take us a way that keeps us in the trees. We'll approach the barn from behind. It's out of the way a few miles, but worth it if we can keep up a good pace."

She eyed his concerned expression and placed a hand on his arm. "Luke, if you turn around and follow the stream, it'll take you right to the fence in a little over a mile. It's barbed wire, but I'm sure you could handle it. The road is right next to it. I insist."

Luke exhaled. "I made it clear I'm not going anywhere without you, Gabriella. The faster we can get what you need, the faster I can get you to safety."

She beamed and touched his shoulder. "I'm thankful for you. You were there for me in college when I most needed an honest friend. Even with our awkward history, I knew you were the only real estate developer I could trust."

So much for waiting for better timing. If Luke ignored that opening and found out later, she'd lump him in with every other liar in her life. "Gabriella, I need to tell you something."

Her dark eyes widened. Luke focused on the willow tree ahead. When he looked at her, the beauty and vulnerability threatened to be his undoing. "You think that everything that's happened to us—to you—has stemmed from the media featuring you and your charity, right?"

"Yes. I know. I'm sorry it ever happened. We've already had three times the amount of donations we'd normally have this time of year, which is great, but given the circumstances, so not worth it." She shook her index finger in the air. "I'd like to give that reporter a piece of my mind, and the editor who approved it and the people who read it..."

Luke turned to her. It was obvious she was only venting, but he took the opportunity. "Then you better give it to me."

Her eyes narrowed as she tilted her head. "What do you mean? Are you trying to tell me you're actually a reporter?"

"No." He took a deep breath. "But I do have some contacts in New York. From what I've seen, I thought your foundation was worth some recognition. If they didn't feature you, they'd feature someone else, right? I thought I was doing a good thing. I'm sorry." She remained silent. He met her eyes as she stared at him.

She nodded, turned and stomped toward the willow tree.

"Are you mad?"

"I don't know what I am yet."

He huffed. He could never predict her responses.

She spun to him. "Why? What'd you expect me to say?"

He shrugged, and he knew he should stop talking but couldn't help himself. "I hoped you could acknowledge I tried to do a good thing for you."

She raised her eyebrows. "Is that why you told me then, Luke? To make yourself feel better?"

He threw his hands in the air. He couldn't win, and he hated that they'd still escaped and yet remained in just as much danger as before. "I was trying to be honest. And even if you had a heads-up from me, would you have really turned it down? They'd still have found you."

"Well, if *I'm* being honest, you could've waited until a better time when I could process and handle the news a little better." Her voice cracked.

"Answer me straight up. If I had waited and told you later...first off, I have no idea when that would be, and second, wouldn't you have thought I was lying?"

Her eyes softened. "I don't know."

"Gabriella, I don't want to ever be the guy that lied to you. I know how much honesty means to you, and though I'm doing a rotten job of it, I'm trying." He wanted to lie down, to ease the pain in his hip. Never before had anything good come out of his mouth when he was tired or in pain. "And I'm sorry. I'm exhausted."

She searched his face, and he wished she'd voice her thoughts aloud. She stepped closer, pain mirroring his features. Her eyes widened as she looked past him. "In the trees," she whispered.

Gabriella tugged on his wrist until they were between two lilac trees. She turned into his chest as bees buzzed around their heads. He wrapped his arms around her and stilled. The bees went back to work on the blooming buds. As the smell calmed his pounding heart, he leaned down and whispered into her thick dark hair. "Did you see him?"

She shook her head into the flannel shirt. "No. I saw the arborvitae trees we went through shake." She stiffened in his arms. "I'm allergic to bees, Luke." She flinched again as a bee buzzed from one tree to the next. "Worst place to hide."

Luke held her as he peeked around the corner. Sure enough, Rodrigo had appeared, looking up and down the stream. "If you're allergic, how do you pick berries?" he whispered, hoping to distract her.

"I go early in the morning or late at night. It must be later in the day than I thought."

Great. "Do you have an EpiPen in the house?"

She mumbled into his shirt. He bent his head down low, careful not to jostle any of the branches. "Say again?"

"One in my glove box. But he took the keys, remember?"

He wouldn't forget that anytime soon. *I need some*

wisdom, Lord. Without weapons there wasn't much he could do. A river rock caught his eye. He bent down, which was no easy feat as Gabriella kept her hands and face covered in his shirt. He grabbed the smooth rock. The buzzing seemed quieter near the ground. If he didn't succeed, maybe they could crawl away. Though, clover grew on the other side of the trees— another known bee hangout.

Luke inhaled through his nose to calm his heart and straightened, pulling her up with him so she could keep her face protected.

He needed to pretend he was playing in the church softball league or the stress would mess up his aim. *Just another afternoon beating their rival team, the Swinging Shepherds.* He pulled his arm back, twisted his hips and let the rock fly.

A pulling sensation spread across his thigh. He bit his lip to keep from groaning aloud. Warmth dripped down his leg. Great. He'd ripped the wound back open.

The crackling from the tree branches across the river confirmed he met his mark. Two brown streaks ran in the opposite direction through the dense wooded area. "Deer?"

"What?" She peeked up at him.

He grinned. "I think I scared some deer."

Crack! Crack! Gabriella jerked in his arms. Splashing followed. Rodrigo ran through the water into the forest, chasing after his new friends. "I don't think he could see them from his vantage point. Come on. Before he figures out who he's chasing."

He pulled her out of the lilac trees and they ran until they were under the cover of the willow tree branches.

She hunched over her knees, catching her breath. "You're bleeding again." Her voice went flat.

"Yeah."

"Some pair we make." She beckoned him to step behind the trunk. "I didn't think he would be on to us this soon. I don't want to lead him to the barn, Luke."

"Don't slow down on my account."

"Unless we change our minds and want to run through the field of alfalfa, we're about to get our feet wet." She marched past a group of shrubs, revealing a couple more pools of water.

He marveled at the beauty surrounding him. As she trudged past another group of trees, the sound of a hundred streams of rippling water drew him forward until he spotted the smallest of waterfalls from one hill down to the rocks below surrounded by low-hanging foliage.

A splash set his nerves on edge. "Rainbow trout," she said. Fish larger than most fishermen dreamed of wiggled their way up the tiny waterfall.

He looked over his shoulder and almost hollered at the pair of steely eyes looking at him from a dwarfed tree. "Is that an eagle?"

"Uh...no. That's an osprey." She hit his shoulder and pointed up in the sky where giant wings made a shadow twice as large below. "Now that's an eagle. I wish we could stay and hide here."

A sweet aroma overpowered the smell of forest fires in the west. His stomach roared. A slow, hesitant smile grew on her face. "Good timing."

Gabriella pointed to a spot without shade directly to the south of where they hid. It looked like giant hills of twigs piled high. "One is blackberries, the other raspberries. The raspberries are probably our best bet. If you get the spring batch, the birds and the pests haven't really touched them yet. It should be relatively safe to eat without washing."

"Stay here. We don't need you taking chances with your allergy."

Her shoulders dropped, most likely in relief at his suggestion. He looked all around before darting to the bush. The buzzing confirmed his choice. Although most of the berries looked pink, he tenderly lifted a branch, careful to keep his fingers in the small space between the thorns. His mouth watered at the grouping of luscious red fruit. He filled the flannel pocket and his two hands before hustling back to her in the shelter of the shade.

"Hold out your hand."

She accepted with a smile. "We need to keep moving. Especially since we're taking the long way."

"I think that's wise. Rodrigo is bound to have figured out by now he was chasing deer." Luke threw the remaining berries into his mouth. "Is that enough to hold you, Gabriella?"

The birds sang as she hiked uphill. Her eyes looked wet as she glanced at him. "Besides my mom, you're the only one who calls me by my full name."

"It's what you like though, right?"

She shook her head. "That's the thing. Everyone just calls me Gabbie and doesn't ever ask. How'd you know?"

"I overheard you tell Thad you preferred your given name once."

Her eyes widened. She shook her head. "And you're still single."

The comment hit him the wrong way, although he

wasn't sure why. He couldn't tell if she meant it as a compliment or a dig. "Did you ever get your rebound relationship?" The question slipped out before he could filter it.

She spun around and placed her hands on her hips. "When you say it that way, it makes it sound as if I wanted a rebound."

"I believe your words were, 'I don't want you to be my rebound.' That pretty much implied it."

Her mouth gaped. "You're twisting my words."

"No, that was an exact quote. You remember these things when a girl rejects you after you've kissed her."

She jerked back as if he'd slapped her. "We never kissed!" She huffed. "And, I'd only found out three months before that the person I *thought* was going to stay committed to me for the rest of my life had instead cheated on me." She flung a finger in the air. "Someone just told me it takes five years to get over someone cheating you. Five years! And maybe I didn't need that long, but I needed more time than it took you. I didn't reject you, Luke. I told you I was scared to lose your friendship. I needed it." Her eyes brightened with a moist sheen. "Ironically, I lost that anyway." She turned on her heel and took off.

Luke wished he didn't remember that moment in time so vividly, but he'd held her so tight and as he brushed his lips against hers, she'd stepped away. "If we didn't kiss, what would you call it?" Luke pumped his arms to keep up with her lengthened stride up the hill. His injury made him take two steps for every one of hers.

Gabriella's face reddened. For a split second he worried she'd been stung until she said, "It was a hug, Luke.

We were stepping away from a hug. Believe me, you'll know when I kiss you." She held up a hand, this time her face bright red. "I mean, if I kissed you ever." She shook her head. "Not that I would." She groaned. "Can we just please drop it?"

ELEVEN

Gabriella wished she could roll down the grass hill and pretend she was young, carefree and without worry. If she could do it all over again, she'd do everything differently. Maybe she'd never have disobeyed as a teen, and her mother would feel she could share everything with her, trust Gabriella with her secrets. And somehow this could all be avoided. She'd insist her mother go in for her yearly checkups, and the heart attack that stole her would be prevented. Her mother avoided doctors, as much as law enforcement, so who knew if it could've been stopped without a medical history to examine.

His voice pierced through her thoughts. "But it takes two people to lose a friendship. What am I saying? You never lost my friendship. You avoided me as much as I avoided you. I never chose to stop being your friend."

"It was so easy to be around you before that. You had to push. You had to make it awkward." Anger she thought disappeared long ago resurfaced. Her throat burned. She hated to admit it, but the memory still hurt. The remaining months of college had been lonelier than ever.

"Sometimes the thing we dread discussing is the

conversation we most need to have." He released an ex-aggerated sigh. "Gabriella, I'm sorry. I've never been good at timing. With Rose, with the media thing, with needing some closure between us…"

She frowned. "What do you mean with Rose? How was that bad timing?" Gabriella took a step back and tilted her head. "Wait a second. Did you know about her and Thad before I did?"

He shook his head. "No. I tried to tell you back then, but I didn't handle it well. I had intended to break it off with Rose before we ever found out her and Thad were together behind our backs. And if I had broke up with her, maybe they wouldn't have kept it a secret, and we could have found out in a much less painful way. I've always regretted that."

They reached the second river. She tugged on his shirt to help him keep his balance and led him to the dirt trail next to the bank. "You meant to break it off with Rose earlier? Why?"

He kept his head down, but his eyes darted her way. "I had no idea she was cheating, but something felt off."

"How?"

He rolled his eyes. "You'll think I'm shallow."

She rolled her eyes. "Spill."

"Fine. I knew things weren't right between us when she stopped laughing at my jokes."

Gabriella's breath hitched. She looked away from him so she could wipe the giant smile off her face before he spotted it.

"You're laughing at me, aren't you?"

She shook her head, staring at the skies in hopes she really didn't laugh. "I don't presume to know how guys work, but it just seems a bit cliché."

"How so?"

"Not that you were wrong, but in the future, you know, if you find the right girl... What if your jokes just aren't that funny?"

"Too far."

She turned to find him holding up a finger, but his wide grin assured her he took it how she intended. "My jokes kill."

"Good. You can use them on Rodrigo."

He chuckled, his voice deep and comforting. She instantly regretted not being able to tour the property under different circumstances.

It seemed ironic that laughter could soothe and hurt at the same time. As if she was dehydrated for joy, but when she had some, it reminded her of all the other sorrow in her life. She quickened her step.

Luke sighed. "To put it a better way, when Rose and I were together it was like she'd mentally checked out. Except, of course, when we hung out as couples."

"I'm jealous." She glanced up. "Not that she checked out...that you knew ahead of time. So you could guard your heart." Maybe she'd had him all wrong. Maybe he didn't take relationships flippantly. Was it possible he got over Rose so fast because he had already emotionally distanced himself? Or was the reason he pursued her so soon after the breakup because of loneliness?

"Can I ask you a question?" he blurted. "You started the foundation here, but then you decided to teach in Oregon. Why? Is it because Thad moved here?"

That was the most ridiculous question she'd ever heard. Could it mean he was jealous...of *Thad*? "No. I purposefully didn't keep track of where he went. It's one of the reasons I don't even have a Facebook account. I didn't want the temptation to torture myself with how they were doing."

The wind picked up and blew back her hair. At least it was finally dry. "Believe it or not, I was a really poor student in math in junior high, but my mom and my aunt had what seemed at the time as a natural business sense. Well, apparently we know why now, but anyway—they were responsible for helping it finally click for me. I used to tease Mom that she should be a teacher because she could make math sound exciting. She lit up when explaining the importance of being able to figure out percentages and do multiplication in your head. Then she took me shopping."

Her heart squeezed at the memory. "I never forgot that. I kept thinking about all the other kids in my school that hated math. I wondered if I'd ever have found the dream to teach if I didn't have someone to support me and tutor me like Mom. And most parents don't feel qualified enough to help their kids with advanced math, so…"

"That's why you started the foundation."

She nodded. "And I knew it would have a greater chance to succeed if I based it in a city."

"Then why didn't you move here, too?"

Her gut churned. "I wanted a chance to succeed without my mom." Her voice caught. He had no idea how much she regretted the choice. She would've spent more time with Mom and not cared to prove herself if she could reverse time. "I thought if I taught in the valley it'd be a slap in the face not to live on the property, too."

"Did your mom ever call you on it?"

"No. My great-aunt gave me grief, but not Mom.

I think she understood." Her breath grew shallow. "I hope she understood."

He nodded. "She did."

She raised an eyebrow. How could he possibly know—

"Did you ever end up dating?"

Her neck tingled. Couldn't they just walk without talking?

"Talking keeps my mind off my leg," he said, as if he could hear her thoughts.

"Oh," she stammered. "Um. Yeah. Some. Nothing serious. They didn't really get why teaching and the foundation were so important to me."

He nodded. "They didn't get that your love language is service."

Her eyes widened, and her step faltered at his words. Another gust of wind blew her hair back. The leaves flew off the tree and spun all around them. Luke stepped closer, as if ready to shield her if she needed it. Her throat closed at the gesture. The lightheartedness she experienced only moments ago seemed to blow away with the wind.

Gabriella pointed over his head at the storm clouds building at the top of the foothills to the west. "Looks like we might get rain later."

"Good. Should help lower the risk of you getting stung out here. How much farther to the barn?"

"There will be a sharp bend in the river up ahead. If we walked out of these trees we would need to just run diagonally across the corner of the alfalfa to get to it. Going the long way...maybe a mile left?"

"Do you know why your mom built the barn so far from the house?"

Ah, a safe topic. "Yes. So I guess we lived in the barn

while she started her business and mined a big section of the property. Once she made enough money, she built the house and we moved."

She waved her hand in front of her. "She wasn't done mining the rest of the property, though, so that's why the buildings are so far apart. It had the most land without water features. You'll probably get the most houses out of that portion of property if you decide to develop it." She bit her lip. She hated thinking about the beauty all around turning into subdivisions of cookie-cutter houses.

Luke noticed her eyes turn down every time she mentioned the future possibility of ripping up her beloved property. It would be necessary, sure, but would she look at him like the man that helped her make sure her aunt was taken care of? Or the man that ripped up her mom's pride and joy, her legacy...

Or both?

The beauty around him, despite the horrible situation they found themselves in, was a reminder of God's grace, His majesty, and the fact that Luke could trust Him. And his job basically destroyed all the beautiful creation. People needed places to live, sure, but...

Gabriella slowed her pace and looked at him, as if waiting for a response. But he wasn't ready to share his frustration.

"Did you always know you wanted to teach?" he asked.

She huffed. "Believe it or not, I was aimless."

"You didn't act aimless."

"I didn't want to disappoint my mom. I didn't want her to feel bad that all I ever wanted was to be a wife and mom. She never had that. Maybe it's because I grew up without a father. I don't really think that's why, but I'm sure someone could make the case." Her eyebrows rose as her eyes widened and her jaw went slack. She dipped her chin to her chest. "I've never told anyone that."

He shrugged. "Really? Why not? What's the big deal of sharing you wanted a family someday?"

She shook her head. "Because I also wanted to be independent. If I told people that—" her eyes darted toward him "—they might get the wrong idea."

Luke almost laughed. In other words, she worried he'd take it as a pickup line. And even if he was delusional enough to think that, it seemed clear she didn't like the idea. His leg ached with each step, and another trickle of blood slipped down his thigh. The conversation wasn't helping him keep his mind off the pain anymore.

Five feet ahead a collection of boulders sat in the middle of the trail. She stopped. "I'd forgotten about these."

"What are they?"

"Once a year, on Easter, we would go on a family hike and go down this trail. Mom loved spring because it reminded her of new beginnings and a new life in Christ."

Her mouth twisted to the side. "We didn't do it this year. They visited me in Oregon because I had too much grading to catch up on to drive here for the weekend. I was so selfish." Her entire life had been cast with a different light. Where once she thought her classwork of the ultimate importance, now she'd give it all up just to have another hike.

"Gabriella, you weren't selfish. You were trying to be responsible. Your mom knew that. It's why she came to you instead."

She brushed away the tears. "Yeah, maybe." She glanced at Luke. "Are you familiar with the story of Joshua and the Jordan?"

His lips shifted to the side. "Um…"

She thought as much. "Sunday school makes sure most people remember the parting of the Red Sea, but my mom's favorite story is in the Old Testament, when Joshua needs to lead the people across the Jordan River. When the feet of the priests who carried the ark touched the water, it parted, and all the people crossed the Jordan on dry land."

The story her mom had told so many times lightened her mood. "Once everyone crossed, they were to pick out twelve stones—"

"So when their children asked their fathers what the stones were all about, they could share what the Lord had done for them."

She grinned. "You do remember." They reached the stones, although they almost qualified as boulders. "So during the mining, whenever they found these giant ones, Mom had the guys move them here. After she collected twelve, she sold the rest for landscape purposes."

Gabriella stepped up on the first one, two feet above the ground. "I used to pretend I was on top of a mountain range and hop from one to the next one. Scared my mom to death." Cold rushed through her veins at the realization of what she'd just said. She'd never given the common expression a second thought until now.

"Are you saying your mom put these here so she could tell you what God had done for her?"

The change of subject felt like a slap in the face. "Yes." Her memories seemed to be playing in fast-forward through her mind. Except now, with the new knowledge…

"Luke, I never really understood the significance until now. Maybe she put these here as a reminder of how God saved her, my aunt and me from the life of the mafia…from death."

A movement to her right, through the swaying leaves, caught her attention. She froze and hoped the man wading through the alfalfa next to the line of trees hadn't seen them. He appeared to be a couple of acres away, looking left to right. "Luke," she whispered. "He definitely figured out we weren't deer."

"Which way is he going?"

"He's following the same line of trees around the field that we did. Only he's just a mile or two behind us."

A sudden wind gust propelled Gabriella forward. Luke reached out and caught her as she slipped head-first. She strained against his arm that pressed into her abdomen to right herself. Her heart raced at the thought of the pain she would've experienced had she crashed into the next stone. "That was out of the blue," she started to say.

Crack!

She couldn't see where the bullet had gone, but the sound was unmistakable. They'd been spotted.

She looked up at Luke, but the giant wall of darkness in the distance took her breath away.

TWELVE

Luke flinched at the sound of the gunshot. Gabriella's wide eyes seemed more terrified of whatever lurked behind him. He followed the path of her gaze.

Above the foothills, the sky turned into a massive front of swirling red and gray hues. It reached as high as he could see, as if there were no end to it. His grip on Gabriella tightened as he lifted her up and set her down on the ground beside him, behind a tree where Rodrigo couldn't see them.

Except the trees all bent with the force of the sustained winds. Leaves and twigs rained down. His heart jumped to his throat. The last thing he wanted to do was to run and test the wound in his leg further, but it looked as if they had no choice. "It's a dust storm. We need to get to that barn…now."

Her eyes widened, and she trembled, clinging to him. They needed to get to shelter before the winds brought the choking sand and blinding dust any closer.

Luke should've recognized the signs. When fires raged in the west, an impending storm traveled their way and the early morning air stayed below fifty degrees, it made the conditions ripe for what they called a "haboob."

While dust storms weren't uncommon in the area, Luke had always been inside when one was about to hit, especially one of this magnitude. Seeing something that resembled a tsunami of dirt about to wash over the land filled him with a combination of awe and terror. Right now, terror won by leaps and bounds.

Gabriella pulled on his wrist. "I don't think we'll beat it if we stay to the trail."

"What if we cut across the alfalfa like you mentioned earlier?"

"But…but you saw him." Her shaky finger pointed to the trees. "He might see us. Might shoot at us again. And this time, he might meet his mark."

The massive dark coils of dirt and clouds moved closer, over the top ridge of the mountains. "Assuming he has half a brain, he'll be more worried about finding shelter himself." Luke imagined what the stinging bits of dust and sand would feel like against his skin with the intense force of the winds. "I think it's a risk we need to take."

She nodded and moved to an oak tree just beyond the trail of stones. "It's going to be a challenge to keep my bearings. Have you ever run through alfalfa? There are natural rows, but we need to cut diagonally through the corner so the plants are going to hit us more. Stay close. If the dust hits us, grab my hand and we'll hit the ground."

"Let's hope it doesn't come to that."

Gabriella crouched down and took off. Luke hunkered down and pushed off his toes. He almost cried out at the sudden sting of his leg. He narrowed his eyes and focused on Gabriella's thick hair swishing side to side as she ran through the sticky plants.

The alfalfa hit against his legs. The plants whipped his broken skin. He pressed his hand over his wound, gritting his teeth together to forget the pain. The smell of the air filled with leaf oils, hay and dust. The wind shifted slightly and the alfalfa moved as a unit to block their way.

Gabriella slowed. He heard her voice cry out but through the wind couldn't tell what she was saying. Maybe running through the plants hurt her knees? She fell to the ground.

Luke almost tripped and fell on her, but he strained his back, turning to the right, and landed on his side, next to her. A thick branch soared through the air two feet over their heads. He gasped and his lungs seized with coughing. So she'd dropped because of the branch.

Gabriella kept her head down. "I don't know if we can keep going," she yelled.

Luke pulled his shirt over his nose and mouth and peeked behind him. While the air was dusty, the giant mass had turned into a brown wall and had yet to hit the land.

He pulled Gabriella close. "It's coming."

Her head turned as her hand moved her flying hair out of the way. He watched her mauve lips move before he registered what she said: "We have to keep going."

She blinked slowly, watching him until he nodded, then jumped up and set off running through the wind. Luke followed her lead and understood her despair. The wind had to have reached upward of seventy miles an hour. It seemed he was running against an invisible force holding him back. His throat hurt from trying to take a breath. They had to get shelter.

Gabriella's right arm shot out. She pointed to a

grouping of bent trees. Through the hazy sky he could make it out—the barn! Her pace slowed but judging by the way she pumped her arms, he realized running against the wind and the plants proved too much for her. Luke dared a look over his shoulder. The swirling had crossed the foothills. It would only be a matter of seconds now.

"Gab—" he tried to shout, but it did no good. She couldn't hear over the noise. Splattering of moisture slapped his face. Rain or escaped droplets from the many creeks, ponds and the lake?

Luke had never been more thankful for his three brothers. They'd trained him for wrestling and tackling, despite his lack of enthusiasm for the sports.

He dipped down. His arm wrapped around Gabriella's frame. She stiffened as he cupped his right hand underneath her knees and swept her up into his arms. As he cradled her against his chest, she turned in to his shirt. She trusted him, and he refused to prove her wrong.

Luke sprinted like never before. His legs pleaded for relief as the alfalfa beat against him and the wind shoved him backward.

A rumble in the distance pushed him faster. Crackling trees and the sound of dirt pelting the ground in the distance drove fear into his spine. Gabriella's arms reached around his neck, clinging to him.

Faster, he needed to go faster. He lengthened his stride as the trees grew closer. Tumbleweed rushed across the field. He hurdled over it and ducked underneath the flailing branches in front of them.

His feet touched dirt. They were out of the alfalfa.

He turned his face as the wind picked up the loose soil, as well.

Gabriella's legs pressed against his arms. She dropped down. They must be close. The sound of rain, like a parade of drumrolls hitting a snare, crescendoed. It hit them from the side, and he tripped and fell over to the ground. Except it wasn't rain. The sand and dust plastered him.

He curled in a ball, wanting to scream out, but Gabriella consumed his thoughts. One painful move at a time, though he couldn't see, he reached where she should be with his fingers. The top of his hands felt beaten by tiny nails as the tips of his fingers reached wood and... what felt like another hand. He grasped it and forced them both to standing. He pulled his shirt over his head and peeked out of his sand-encrusted eyes. Gabriella had found the handle of the door and struggled against the wind to pull on it.

Luke wrapped himself around her back, hoping to shield her as he grabbed the handle and threw his body back. The door opened just enough for Gabriella to slip through. He kicked his wingtips against the door, and though the door slammed against the back of his leg, he managed to slide into the barn.

The darkness forced his other senses into overdrive. The smell of sulfur, mixed with the overwhelming odor of hay and dust and rotting leaves, triggered the gag reflux.

Gabriella's coughs barely reached his ears. His head pounded. The air quality must have done a number on his sinuses. The top of his scalp tingled, and the sensation traveled down his face and body, as if his skin just realized the beating it'd taken.

Gabriella groaned. "It stings. And I'm afraid to open my eyes."

The wind raged. The barn's walls creaked and groaned. He lifted the inside layer of his shirt and wiped off his eyes, then his lips. A layer of dust wouldn't budge, though, as if it'd been spray-washed onto his skin. "Don't forget to brush off your eyebrows and shake out your hair before you open your eyes," he suggested.

One of the walls had a set of windows at chest level. He crossed over, thinking he'd wipe off the dust from the windows with his sleeve, but what good would that do? A good six feet above, near the apex of the roof, another square window provided minimal light. The floor was not dirt as he had imagined it would be, but shiny wooden laminate. While the walls weren't finished, he could imagine the charm of the rustic beams.

"Luke, did Rodrigo see which way we went? Did he follow?"

His gaze remained on the window, waiting for the thick brown air to settle so he could see. "I have no idea."

"Then we can't afford to wait the storm out."

Gabriella shivered. She wanted to jump out of her own skin to get rid of the stinging, scratching feeling of dirt and sand. The wind shook the panes Luke tried to peer out of.

Another round of dirt sprayed against the side. A flash of bright light through the red sky lit up the room. Cement, almost like a sidewalk, lined the outer edges of the barn's main area, but in the center, wood flooring gleamed as if it'd been recently oiled. Thunder boomed, and she jumped.

Luke crossed the room. "This doesn't look like a normal barn."

"No, you're right. I told you we lived here for a little while." She squinted as she looked toward the rafters. Across the expanse, wooden stairs led to a long banister that spanned the length of the building.

"I don't remember, but Mom said she and I shared a bed up there. They took down the curtain just a few years ago that apparently separated her bed and my great-aunt's."

"Seems odd that they'd put beds up there."

Gabriella tilted her head. "That's what I said!" She shook her head. "They acted like I was the crazy one."

"If they were worried about being found, your mom might've wanted that vantage point for a leg up. Assuming there's another exit up there that's easier to find than the one in the safe room."

An uneasy laugh bubbled up. She wanted to forget the near miss of almost suffocating. "There's a fire escape. And I'm pretty sure she had her gun ready and waiting."

"I can't believe she lived here with you as a baby. I mean, I love camping as much as the next guy, but I can't imagine taking care of a baby without a kitchen."

"You're right. We at least had a bathroom." She gasped. "Luke. A bathroom." She crossed the room. Her eyes stung from the tiny sand particles still stuck underneath her lids.

"Aren't you forgetting Rodrigo shut off the water?"

"He shut off the water to the house. He couldn't have

shut off the water to the barn unless he came out here. We have a private well, remember?"

"Don't get my hopes up, Gabriella."

She flicked on the light in the bathroom. A dim glow erupted from the single lightbulb in the middle of the ceiling. The twist of the handle on the sink produced a chugging, popping noise followed by brown water. She tensed, then mercifully, the color lightened and clear water poured out of the faucet. Her fingers dove into the stream, washing away the grime.

Luke slid past her and closed the door. "In case Rodrigo is nearby. We don't want him to see the light." The same choked sound resulted from the bathtub as Luke waited to take advantage of the water at the same time.

One lone hand towel hung from the side wall. Gabriella didn't even want to think how long it'd been since it had been washed or switched. But the smeared mirror revealed it would only take one wrong move before the caked-on dirt would get in her eyes. She dipped her head over the sink and splashed the icy water over her features and began scrubbing, squeezing her eyes tight as she felt the layer slipping off. Then she cupped the water in her hand and blinked into the small pool of water until the stinging vanished. She repeated the process with her other eye.

How she wished she had time for a shower and the ability to forget about Rodrigo and the men who had her great-aunt's life in their hands.

She reached for the towel blindly and opened it to the underside before patting her face dry.

"Can you pass that over when you're done?"

Gabriella held it out to him as she firmly pressed her

lips closed. She prevented voicing her thoughts on just how many germs likely flourished on that towel. He straightened, and she no longer cared. His clean face brought comfort.

The thunder shook the mirror on the wall, followed by the pounding of rain. His gaze met hers in the mirror, and a sudden vulnerability overwhelmed her.

"It feels hopeless," she whispered. How did she ever think she could win against the mafia?

"Hey, don't say that." His voice lowered, and he placed a hand on her shoulder.

Her chin dropped. "I should've listened to you and gone straight to the police. I just didn't want to risk it. They said if they found out, they'd kill her on the spot." Her eyes burned and her vision blurred. She'd failed. "But you were right, Luke. She would've at least had a chance instead of none—" her throat closed "—at all."

Luke's hands framed her face as his thumb brushed the tear off her cheek. She lifted her eyes. How was it that he could make her feel safe and terrified all at the same time? She inhaled in hopes her ribs would expand enough that he wouldn't hear her heart beating against them.

"If it were my own mom, I'm not sure I would've been able to risk it either. And time isn't up, Gabriella."

The way he said her name soothed her in a way nothing else but hot cocoa and a hug from her mom did. Her mind cleared. If she gave up now, she'd never forgive herself. "Keep fighting until time runs out, right?"

"Nothing is impossible with God."

She took a shaky breath. She loved that verse, although at times she found it confusing. It didn't proclaim a promise that everything would work out the way she wanted, but the very words were infused with hope. God was more powerful than the mafia, than the situation—and she didn't want to admit it aloud because it scared her too much—but she knew in her heart that He was even more powerful than death.

Gabriella pulled back her shoulders. "I really needed to hear that."

Luke nodded. "I did, too." His chin tilted to the ceiling. "Hopefully the rain is clearing the air." He reached around her and flicked off the light.

She flinched as the room plunged in darkness.

"Sorry. I didn't want to bring any attention to us when I open the door. I should've warned you."

"I understand." She hated the way her voice sounded weak and wimpy. Her great-aunt was counting on her acting brave, not cowering because of the darkness.

His arm brushed past hers. The squeak of metal meant he was opening the door. She stepped closer to the sink as the door swung inward. "If you lived upstairs, any chance your mom left you anything there?"

Gabriella couldn't imagine that would be the case. Although she still wasn't sure if going to the barn was a wild-goose chase. Would her mom really have tried to indicate a clue by describing the barn as historic?

Her gut twisted with threatening despair. It wasn't as if she had anything else to go on. "Your guess is as good as mine," she answered.

The sound of their footsteps in the cavernous room echoed like a poorly synchronized rhythm section, accompanying the rain's melody. Her eyes adjusted, but she could still only make out the outline of the stairway in front of them. "Stay to the right, otherwise you might fall downstairs."

Luke turned. "Downstairs?"

"There's a cellar down there. Pure dirt floor. Mom used it for storing things."

"Sounds like the place to start."

"It's been empty for years." A chill ran up her spine as she thought about the tens…maybe hundreds of spiders and who knew what else that had time to move into the dank room. "Besides, we don't have a flashlight."

"There's no light down there?"

"I don't think so. There's a lightbulb at the bottom of the steps but nothing to keep Rodrigo from seeing it outside if he's nearby."

Luke reached for her wrist. "I think we at least have to rule out the possibility, Gabriella. You want to wait here while I check it out?"

She hated both options, but the thought of being alone if Rodrigo stormed through the door caused her to tremble more than the image of spiders and mice. "No, I'm coming, but I won't object to you leading the way."

The dark outline of his profile turned and as his head dipped, she knew he was descending the steps. She shoved her foot in front of her to feel for the frame of the step before going down. With one hand out, she stopped at the touch of Luke's back.

"I found the light switch," he said. "I'm going to flip it on and take a quick look. You ready?"

She nodded but realized he couldn't see her. "Yes."

The light blinded her momentarily as the cellar door swung open. The beam reflected off many shiny surfaces. Gabriella squinted, trying to process what she saw. The room also seemed longer than she remembered… and less dirt packed.

"Uh…Gabriella. I don't think this is a cellar anymore." Luke felt around the corner and beautiful, bright light from actual fixtures filled the long room.

Her mouth dropped. "No. It's a shooting range."

THIRTEEN

Luke flipped off the stairway light and stepped fully inside the room.

He'd seen underground shooting ranges before but never underneath a barn. A floor epoxy made the walls gleam. The horizontal lines spread out in intervals labeled the yards.

Her mom must have really wanted to make sure she was a great shot no matter how close or far she stood from the target. The walls looked to be covered in sound-absorbent panels. Judging by the rectangular lines that didn't match the rest of the panels, they covered up the egress windows. And, if she knew what she was doing, and Luke had no reason to believe she didn't, the walls underneath the paneling would've been made with twelve-inch, sand-filled blocks.

His gaze moved to the ceiling: pre-stressed planking topped with four inches of steel-reinforced concrete. Fully enclosed bullet traps were placed just beyond the paper targets.

Directly to the right sat a leather recliner, a side table, and a mini fridge. He grunted. Add a television and this would be the ultimate man cave.

He walked to the boxes of ammunition carefully stacked on a gray waist-high countertop. Jacketed and plated bullets were the only selection. Why? The answer hit him immediately. Lead bullets would lead to gun smoke and airborne residue. "Your mom was one smart lady."

He turned to find Gabriella's face white and chalky, her eyes filled with horror. "What did you say?"

Luke instantly regretted his comment. He tried to pull her into a hug, but she pushed him away, her face flushing.

"Her whole life was a lie. I've been trying to avoid thinking about it, avoid being furious at her, but this… this was the last straw. She put me in this situation, where I have nothing to go on to try to save my aunt. Our own lives are in danger. You've been shot."

She spun away, and her shoulders rose and fell. "I loved my mom dearly and I will miss her every single day, but this…this secret life she had…" Gabriella shook her head. "No. 'Smart lady' wasn't the first thing that came to mind."

Her whole body trembled as she flung her hand out, gesturing at the room. "Why'd she keep this secret anyway? What harm would it have done if she'd told me? Showed me?"

Luke hung his head. He imagined he'd be offended, too, if in her situation. "You're right," he said. "I was speaking as someone who appreciates good construction and design."

Her rigid stance and clenched jaw softened. "No, you were referring to the recliner and the mini fridge." She smirked, and he knew that if she was attempting a joke, she'd forgiven him.

"It doesn't hurt." His dry mouth and burning throat begged to be relieved. He could still taste the dust particles that refused to leave on their own. "Let's pray there is something drinkable in there and start looking for that evidence."

He crossed to the fridge and fought against the temptation to sit in the soft leather. It looked so relaxing. If he succumbed, he knew it would make it almost impossible to get back up. His leg throbbed at the thought of relief.

He gaped at the contents of the fridge and almost verbally complimented her mom's taste again. "Look, Gabriella. Your favorite." He held up a cold can of Pibb Xtra.

Her forehead crinkled, but she approached and accepted. The rest of the options were diet, so Luke pulled out a Pibb for himself, as well. "Must have been your mom's favorite, too, huh?"

She shook her head, popped the can and the beautiful hissing of air and popping fizz filled the space between them. Luke opened his and downed half the can in one smooth gulp. He hit his fist against his chest in hopes of helping the swallowed air escape in a gentlemanlike fashion.

Gabriella gulped down her share and exhaled. "That's just it." She shook her head. "Mom only drank diet. This was my favorite drink." She raised an eyebrow. "I can't believe you remembered, though."

He shrugged. "I was an impressionable young man. I remember a lot of things." His mind filled with all the moments and conversations they'd shared in college. Their eyes met, and the air between them seemed charged with electricity.

He looked down the range so as to keep his mind focused. "So there's only one explanation for your favorite drink being stocked down here. Your mom must've been preparing to share this with you."

She nodded. "Maybe."

Luke set his can down on the cabinet. "If she had shown you this shooting range before, you would've picked up on the historic reference in the will right away, right?"

Her eyes widened.

He brushed away an obvious clump of dust he hadn't seen before on his shirt. "Right. So, humor me and let's assume she had hoped to show you this place. And in that case, the historic reference to the barn would be an obvious clue, so we're on the right track."

Gabriella drew in her eyebrows. "Huh. You might be right."

Luke put a finger on his lip while his thumb held up his chin, a habitual gesture when he needed to process. So he likely hadn't been dreaming when Gabriella's mother mentioned she'd done something with the barn in the diary. And if that was the case, what better place to hide the evidence? He looked around the room. "If it were me, and I needed to keep something safe…" He dropped his hands at the last word. "I'd put it in the gun safe."

Gabriella curled her lip. "Really?"

He nodded. "Yep."

They approached the six-foot, hunter-green gun safe. The gold accents lined the edges of the matte finish. In the center a long gold handle resided just underneath a black combination dial. Gabriella's fingers reached for the dial and stopped.

"What should I try?" she whispered.

"Stick with five- or six-digit combinations that you think would be important to your mom."

Gabriella bit her lip and spun the dial to the right, then left, then back right.

Her hand drifted to the handle. But it wouldn't budge. She tried again with the same result.

"Talk me through it," Luke said.

"I've tried her birthday, Aunt Freddie's birthday..." She growled. "If those were even their real birthdays." Gabriella pulled her long hair off her back, twirled it around her hand and tucked it back through the space she'd created. Her graceful movements and the resulting ponytail transfixed him, like origami with hair.

"Try your birthday," he suggested. "She'd have picked a combination you'd know."

She stared at him for a moment before she shook her head in disbelief. "Okay."

Her wrist whipped through the combination. She slipped her hand to the handle and exhaled. *Click.* A radiant smile crossed her face before it morphed into sober concern. "If it's not here, I won't know where else to look."

"You're not alone," he said.

She pulled the seal. Inside were a few guns, but most of the twenty-four slots were empty. Instead, a thick beige canvas bag sat propped up on its side...except the zipper had a key sticking out of it.

"It's a deposit bag," Luke said.

Gabriella's shaking hand reached and turned it and began to unzip.

Her entire arm trembled when she opened it.

Stacks of documents and small cassette tapes filled the bag. On top, though, sat a single white envelope

with Gabriella's name in black marker. She placed a
hand on her chest. Her face paled, but she didn't make
a move to pick the bag up.

If reading her mother's diary proved to be almost
impossible, Luke imagined a direct letter to her would
prove that much more difficult. "Shall I?" he asked.

She nodded.

He pulled out the stationery lined in flowers from
the envelope and began to read aloud:

"Dear Gabriella,
"If you are reading this I'm truly sorry, honey. It
most likely means I've failed, left you in a horrible mess and owe you an explanation. I can only
hope it will lead to your forgiveness."

"Yeah, she did," Gabriella muttered. She wrapped
her arms around herself, said nothing, but nodded for
him to continue.

"I've been Samantha Radcliffe for so long it's
as if Renata Mirabella doesn't exist anymore. At
least I wished she didn't. Enough regrets.
"Here's what you need to know:
"I was born into the Mirabella crime family.
My mother never married my father—in fact she
refused him, not wanting to be a part of that life.
Shortly after I was born, they put a hit on her.
My father claimed ownership over me, but your
great-aunt raised me. I have no memories of my
mother or my grandmother on her side, but your
aunt Freddie told me she came from a good family. I wish I—we—had a chance to get to know

them, but I'm so thankful that they willed this property to me and that no one knew about it... except your aunt."

Luke processed the words. So her mother likely owned the property legally. What a relief. Gabriella peered over his shoulder, reading along. "She never met her mother? My grandfather killed her? What kind of person does such a thing?" Gabriella leaned back, shaking her head, but gestured at the letter. Luke kept reading.

"I grew up having to work for my father and uncle. I hope you never meet Uncle Claudio. He's a cruel man, as most all the men in the Mirabella family. My own father did something the family didn't like, and they killed him for it, without hesitation.

"A year before you were born, I was assigned to a man—an honest man from the Treasury Department. My job was to get information from him to help the family get a score of coins from the nineteen hundreds at the US Mint. Only, I fell in love. When I found out about you, it became clear that no one would benefit from the situation."

Gabriella placed a hand on her mouth and squeezed her eyes shut.

"Had you known about your father?"

"She—Mom said he didn't know about me and said it'd be better if it stayed that way. She always prefaced it by telling me to be careful about the company I kept. I assumed she meant my father lived as a druggie or something, not an honest man. I mean, obviously he wasn't perfect, but I always wondered about him… It's part of the reason I kept sneaking into her diary when I was little to look for clues." She eyed the letter. "Is there more?"

He nodded.

"Aunt Freddie was my only confidante. She told me about a mob girlfriend from history—Virginia Hill. She kept a little black diary, where she recorded the money laundering flow. She put it in a safe-deposit box and told the family that upon her death it would be sent to the FBI. In response, they sent her money and left her alone.

"Inspired, I took evidence I'd gathered about who killed my father and copies of all the bookkeeping I'd done for the family. I left a note similar to what I imagine Virginia had left. Your aunt gladly came with me.

"Only, I studied my history after we got here, Gabriella. Virginia's little black book never helped her. Instead it made her a target to the FBI herself. And she ended up dead from an overdose of sleeping pills after the FBI refused to make a deal for the book…a suicide that reeks of a mafia hit to me.

"So instead, the evidence rests here, while we stay hidden underneath our secret identities, waiting until the right time when I'm sure we can be safe. I didn't want to raise you in witness protection—I had a cousin die on her way to WITSEC—I couldn't be sure they wouldn't get us."

Gabriella set the bag on the countertop and began pulling out the documents and tapes as if they were priceless artifacts. "That's why she didn't use a safe-deposit box. My mom has always done the unexpected, thought outside the box." She cringed. "Pun unintended. Go on."

"My hope is they'll never find you. As far as I know, they don't even have word of your existence. I pray it stays that way.

"Please forgive me. This heavy burden on my heart grows daily. I am desperate to tell you but want it to be for the right reasons, not to just ease my own burden. I hope you understand now why I discouraged you from starting the nonprofit. I didn't want to put you in an even worse position someday, tarnishing your reputation. But I soon realized that I couldn't do that to you. I couldn't stop your servant heart. It's a blessing to me, and tangible proof that you were brought up outside of the Mirabella family, away from the suppressing darkness."

Luke could barely read the words. His throat burned, thankful and heartbroken for Gabriella at the same time.

"I am so thankful for you, Gabriella.

"Do what you will with the items in this safe. Choose wisely. Find someone trustworthy. Stay safe. I love you.

"Yours Forever,

"Mom

"PS: I also took the score from the Treasury De-

partment as added insurance. Only you know
where it is. When the time is right, please return
it with my apologies."

Gabriella looked up, raw with emotion. Luke still
held the letter but opened his arms ever so slightly.
She clung to him and buried her face against his chest,
desperate to disappear, to lose herself, until the sand
particles on his shirt scratched her cheek. The prickly
sensation snapped her back to reality. Yes, her mother
had to grow up in a life no one should be forced to endure. And, mercifully, Gabriella had been wrong about
her mom's view of her. She hadn't disapproved of her
servant heart, but quite the opposite. What must it have
been like for Mom to watch her growing up? Did Mom
wonder how she would've turned out growing up away
from the mafia?

Luke's uninjured arm wrapped around her back. His
hand awkwardly patted the back of her head. Her cheek
bounced off his chest, and she reached her hands up and
pushed herself back. "Thank you."

There was no time to grieve. She had to shut off her
mind and act. Her mom had said to do what she would
with the evidence, so she'd feel no guilt handing it over
in exchange for her aunt.

"Your mom risked everything to get this evidence.
We can't just hand it all over," Luke said.

"She never would've wanted my aunt's life to be in
danger, either," she spat out. He didn't respond.

She dug her fingers underneath everything in the bag
and pulled it out and set it in the middle of the countertop. She placed the microtapes and the player to the side.
Inside a manila envelope, photographs stamped with

dates were arranged by size, seemingly taken through a window of men congregating. Gabriella didn't understand the significance, but surely someone else would. She set a ledger and a stack of financial documents to the side.

Luke picked up a black ledger. "May I?"

She nodded her assent and continued her task. Her legs twitched as adrenaline coursed through her veins. Every heartbeat reminded her of the clock ticking. Her mind wasn't processing as fast as she'd like.

The next stack was... Gabriella gasped at the stack of duplicate passports and birth certificates. She flipped open the first. Her mother, pictured in her early forties, stared back at her. Gabriella would likely look exactly like that in the future. When her mother had taken to calling her mini-me, Gabriella would quip back, "No, you're my big-me." Her mother's boisterous laugh would always follow.

The next one took her breath away. She opened the navy leather passport complete with a photograph of Gabriella in her teen years. Her mom must've prepared these in case they needed to go on the run. Otherwise, why wouldn't she have showed her?

As a teen, Gabriella would've loved knowing she had a passport and likely would've showed it off to her friends. Ah, maybe she'd just answered her own question.

Underneath the passport were two birth certificates, one listed as Radcliffe but the other as...

"Gabriella Mirabella?" She dropped it and turned to Luke. "My real name is Gabriella Mirabella?" Her voice rose, but she couldn't control it. "Why couldn't she have at least used my father's name? Whatever that may have been. Surely it'd have been better than Gabriella Mirabella."

"Some people would like a rhyming name…if they wanted to have their name in a rap, or a greeting card?"

"Really?" She put her hands on her hips. "Who? Who would want that, Luke? It's not just a rhyming name, it's a crime family name." She threw up her hands. "I don't even know who I am anymore," she whispered.

He set down the ledger and turned to her. "You know who you are. You are the girl who loves the Lord and loves others."

Luke placed his hands on either side of her shoulders but looked at the ceiling. "When Jesus washed the disciples' feet, when he told them to love one another, he had just done something that the disciples would've never done for each other."

His gaze shifted to meet hers. "That's how I think of you. You serve others in a way that very few would ever do. Because when you serve, you keep your eyes on Jesus." He stepped closer. "If you can't remember who you are, go to Him to remind you. He's the only one that matters."

Her vision blurred. The words he'd said reached her to the core. Luke knew who she was. He knew her heart, and he knew exactly how to set her straight. She blinked rapidly so the tears wouldn't escape. "You understand." Her words came out hushed.

He sighed. "I've been fighting with my own path lately. And even in the worst circumstances, spending time with you again reminded me that I was looking in all the wrong places. I should be thanking you, Gabriella."

The way he said her name… His gentle hands on her

shoulders sent a spark down her arms. She shivered and took another step into the small space separating them. She lifted her arms and intertwined her fingers around the back of his neck. His eyes widened, but he said nothing. His blue eyes stared right into hers, questioning. She stared boldly back and lifted her chin.

Her lips tingled as he pressed his mouth onto hers. His hands dropped to her waist and pulled her closer. Never before had she been kissed with such restrained passion. Her heart stopped for half a second. When he released her she gasped.

He moved his grasp back to her shoulders, as if making sure she would remain steady. Luke looked to the ground. "I guess that's what you meant."

"Wh-what?"

"When you said I'd know if you kissed me."

She spun around to prevent him from seeing her embarrassment. Why'd she ever let herself say such a thing? She knew he was trying to lighten the tension, but she couldn't think of a single witty comeback. "No one should ever be quoted when they're running for their lives."

"Gabriella, I regret trying to rush our relationship in college. You have no idea how much. I've missed our friendship. I've missed you." He exhaled. "And if it makes any difference," he continued, "your mom knew who you really were, too."

His words both soothed and stung. "If I hadn't left her diary in that safe room, maybe I'd have understood *her* more."

"I don't think you would have. The letter did the best job of that."

She looked over her shoulder. "What makes you say that?"

He glanced in every direction but hers. "Because I read the journal while you slept."

Her stomach turned to lava. "You did what?"

Luke's eyes widened. "I was trying to help. You couldn't read it without—you know—you couldn't even read the letter."

She clenched her fists. He'd read what was meant for her. Who knew what private, personal, secret things he knew about her from reading her mom's diary? A letter was so different than a diary. What had her mother said?

Luke reached for her, but she stepped back. "I'm sorry," he said. "If you're worried about anything embarrassing, there wasn't. She spent a fair amount of time talking about her business, believe it or not. She did mention how proud she was of you. Over and over again. She also said something about what she'd done to the barn. I wasn't positive until now, but I'm sure now she was preparing to tell you all about this."

Gabriella turned back to the papers. Her head spun with so many emotions she didn't know what to do. She needed to pick and choose what to offer the mafia in exchange for her aunt, but how could she? Because as bold as she made herself sound, Gabriella knew she wouldn't be able to give it all back to them. The risk and sacrifices her mother took to ensure her safety wasn't lost on her.

In her peripheral vision, Luke picked up the ledger and likewise went back to work. He turned a page and paused midturn. "She said you lived up to your name."

Gabriella stiffened. What did that mean? That she lived up to the Mirabella name or the Radcliffe name?

"You know Gabriella means heroine of God, right? That's what the journal said."

Her heart pounded so hard against her ribs it had to be audible to Luke. Heroine of God? Her mom had named her that? And thought she'd lived up to it? Her eyes burned with withheld emotion. She scoffed and shrugged. "Seems like I couldn't be..."

A creak above stilled them both, shocking the emotion to the farthest recesses of her heart. "Someone's upstairs?"

"You know how to shoot?" he whispered.

She nodded. Her mother had made sure she knew how to operate a gun. But Gabriella's targets had never been anything as fancy as the shooting range. Instead, as a teenager she'd shot tin cans in the pasture, after the fields of alfalfa had been harvested.

"Good." He picked up the box of ammo. "I might have a plan."

FOURTEEN

Gabriella grabbed the letter from her mom and shoved it in her pocket as Luke lined up the guns on the countertop. Her lightning fingers loaded the guns, thanks to her mom's training.

"I still think you should be the one in hiding."

Another creak upstairs prompted her muscles to tense. "I'm not changing my mind. You're of no use to him. He'd shoot first," she hissed.

He narrowed his eyes. Another creak. His eyes darted to the basement door. Rodrigo must be coming down to investigate. "Fine." He grabbed a weapon and disappeared to his hiding place.

She slipped the cold metal under her back waistband and flipped the back of the shirt over it as the door flung open. A surge of nausea washed over her. Could she follow through with the hasty plan? Did she have enough guts to pull it off?

She closed her eyes. *Help me.* Gabriella flung her hands in the air and flashed her eyes open. "Don't shoot! I surrender."

Rodrigo stepped into the room. If he'd found the bathroom upstairs, he hadn't stopped to wash his face.

His face looked brown from the caked-on dust. The bushy eyebrows held the majority of the dirt, though, and must have served to protect his vision. The dust-plastered face didn't hide a raised red ring the size of a cantaloupe in the center of his forehead. She recoiled. Had the fire extinguisher done that?

Her right hand twitched, almost begging to reach for the gun. Without any weapons in her hand, she felt exposed, vulnerable.

Rodrigo's eyes darted around the room. "Where is he?"

"You shot him." It wasn't a lie.

He leveled his aim at her. "I should kill you now. Slowly. Starting with—"

"I found the evidence you wanted," she blurted. Avoidance and distraction were her only allies. The last thing Gabriella wanted to hear was the manner of death Rodrigo imagined for her. She jutted her chin in the direction of the gun cabinet.

Rodrigo shifted. He lowered the gun slightly. "You found it? Good." He stepped forward and without touching, perused the stacks laid out on the countertop.

Gabriella held her breath. She needed him to let his guard down, to pick up the papers. "It's all there," she said.

"Is there a map?"

She frowned, taken off guard. "Uh…a what?"

"I know about the coins." He shoved his index finger on top of the tallest stack. "And I don't see the coins. Where are they?" Rodrigo stiffened and leveled the gun until the aim fell back on her forehead.

Gabriella shook her head. The plan had failed. "You never said anything about coins. Benito never said—"

"I've told you before I don't care what Benito said," Rodrigo roared. "He doesn't know about the score. Your uncle passed that on to me. *Only* to me. He wanted me in charge, not that weasel. I need both to get back my rightful place, and you're going to get it for me."

Rodrigo moved closer, a menacing grin spreading across his face. "I think you know where it is." He raised an eyebrow. "Something in that stack gave you a clue, didn't it, honey?"

The dangerous gleam in his eyes accompanied by the term of endearment sent an involuntary shiver down her spine. She took a step backward, and her back bumped against the gun safe. The metal in her back waistband pushed into her flesh enough to make her cry out. Rodrigo tilted his chin, confused at her exclamation of pain. "I don't know. I haven't had much time to look at the papers."

Luke sprang from his hiding place, a gun leveled on Rodrigo's back. Oh no. It wasn't time yet.

"Drop it," Luke yelled.

Rodrigo spun so fast Luke had no time to react. *Crack!*

The bullet pierced Luke's left shoulder. He slammed against the back wall. His features crumpled, but he still gripped the gun in his right hand.

Rodrigo's fingertips grabbed the back of her neck and shoved her half in front of him as he aimed his own weapon at Gabriella's temple. His left hand moved around her back and gripped her shoulder. "Make another move and she dies."

Her teeth chattered. Her bones trembled. They'd lost.

Luke's eyes widened, full of rage and indecision. Whatever he did, he couldn't lower his weapon. She could accept dying, but Luke needed to get out alive. This was her fault, all her fault. Her misguided stubborn agenda hadn't saved her aunt. She couldn't bear it if it killed another innocent person.

Gabriella balled her hands up in fists and tensed every muscle in her body until she regained control of her emotions. Her mother had forced her to take self-defense classes every summer from high school through college. Maybe for such a time as this.

"Was this the kind of life my mom grew up with? The life you grew up with?" Gabriella challenged. Her voice shook, but she needed time. Time to clear her head.

Rodrigo laughed. "I chose this life, darling. And as soon as I get what I want, it's going to be pretty good. Now, whether you're alive or not is up to your little boyfriend here." He jutted his chin toward Luke as he took a slight sidestep. Only the left side of his body remained behind her. "Lower your weapon or she dies," he said. "Then you're next."

"What about my mom?" Gabriella pressed. "Did she choose it?"

Rodrigo's arms stiffened against her back. "Seems she did all right for herself, now doesn't it? Not everyone gets raised like a princess, like you." His voice shook with rage. It was a wonder he didn't spit. He shoved the tip of the gun harder into her temple. She pulled her head away from the stinging, but Rodrigo only pressed deeper. She cried out.

"Enough," Luke yelled. His face paled.

No. She couldn't let Luke surrender. The moment he dropped the gun, Rodrigo would shoot him dead. *Please, God, no.*

Luke dropped the gun. It clanged against the ground. Rodrigo loosened his hold and shifted his own gun away from Gabriella's temple, moving it toward his new aim. Luke held his arms out, renounced.

The mafia wouldn't take another person she loved!

She twisted her hips, shoving her right foot behind Rodrigo's left. Her kneecap connected with the back of his lower thigh while her hip vaulted his center of gravity forward. At the same time, Gabriella shoved her right elbow into Rodrigo's torso.

He cried out, but the momentum of her move threw his torso backward, over her knee, to the ground. The gun flew out of his hand, and a bullet shot into the ceiling.

Luke's eyes widened and he dropped, presumably to grab his own weapon. At least she hoped it was to do that and not due to the bullet in his shoulder.

Gabriella hopped backward before Rodrigo could grab her legs. Her right hand grabbed the gun from the back of her pants and aimed it at Rodrigo's outstretched hand. "Don't even go for your weapon, or I won't hesitate to shoot you."

Rodrigo composed his slack jaw and narrowed his eyes. "I'm supposed to believe that?"

Why wouldn't he believe it, as they were standing in her mother's shooting range? Ridiculous. Maybe Rodrigo's attitude explained why her mother was so hard on Gabriella about doing her best, pushing herself and always exceeding expectations. Her mom had likely lived most of her life with the men in her family belittling her abilities. Gabriella reached with her left hand to the other gun stuck in the front of her waistband.

She kept her eyes locked on Rodrigo. "Please stay down a second, Luke." In her peripheral vision she could see the paper target to the left. She twisted her left arm and shot three rounds, then moved the second gun to aim at Rodrigo's chest.

His eyes widened and his arm pulled back from its current trajectory.

"You said my mom was a wily one," Gabriella said. "Well, she raised her daughter to be the same way. With the added bonus of making sure I was always overprepared and extra cautious."

Rodrigo glared at her but remained silent.

"Luke?" she called out.

His shadow crossed in front of her. Good. He could stand. "Get his weapon?" she asked. Luke kicked it to the far corner of the room instead of picking it up. Did that mean he was scared to use his left hand?

"Are you okay?"

He moved his fist—gun still in hand—to provide pressure to his left shoulder. "I've been better, but I think I'll live."

Gabriella peeked. Three bullet holes had hit the center target. Muscle memory had worked to her advantage.

"I noticed some rope upstairs," she said.

Luke nodded. "Good idea."

Gabriella nodded at Rodrigo. "We need to finish our little chat. Upstairs. Now."

The moment Rodrigo stood and headed for the door, Gabriella's blood pressure spiked. They were about to enter the darkness, and Rodrigo was twice her size. What was the likelihood he would cooperate?

"Stop," she ordered. Rodrigo turned around. "Luke, can you hold him here while I get the rope?"

His face paled slightly, but he nodded. She sprinted upstairs and grabbed the rope hanging on one of the beams. She flipped on the bathroom light and looked under the sink cabinet. An old plastic box still held a first-aid kit. For all she knew everything in it had probably passed its usefulness. She sighed. Beggars couldn't be choosers.

At the sound of a holler she held her gun out and jogged back downstairs. Rodrigo sat on the floor once again, holding his head. Two feet away sat a fizzing but unopened can of soda.

Luke had a gun pointed at Rodrigo. "He tried to make a move when I bent down for another drink."

Gabriella's gaze drifted to the knife sticking in the wall, a foot above the mini refrigerator. She blinked. So Luke had used the can of pop as a self-defense move. "Resourceful," she muttered. "You're blessed he didn't shoot you," she told Rodrigo.

Luke half smiled in response. "If he came one step closer, that would've been next." The red circle on the edge of his shoulder increased in circumference by the minute. It proved hard to look away. He grabbed his drink. "I can't seem to drink enough."

She dropped the first-aid kit at her feet. Rodrigo needed to be neutralized before she could think straight enough to help Luke. The excessive thirst wasn't a good sign. He had lost too much blood.

Rodrigo caught sight of the rope in her hands. "Let's not be hasty. We can work out a deal."

"Why should I even talk to you?"

"Because we both know there's no way the Mirabella family is going to let you and your aunt walk away from this."

* * *

Luke blew out a long exhale. The adrenaline must have kept the pain at bay until now. The hard floor looked nice. If only he could lie down and give the dull ache in his shoulder and the sting in his leg a rest. His eyelids drooped, but Gabriella needed him alert.

Her brown eyes stared at him and heat filled his chest. She'd called him resourceful. He wasn't about to let her down now. If she tried to tie Rodrigo up while he stood or even while he was down on the ground, like cop style, that would give Rodrigo too many opportunities to get the upper hand. "He needs to sit in that chair before we secure him."

He kept his left hand lax at his side. Any time he moved those fingers, the throbbing and bleeding increased. But it looked as if he'd need to risk that to tie Rodrigo up.

Gabriella's gaze drifted to his side. "Just talk me through it. Keep the gun pointed at Rodrigo. If he gives me any trouble, shoot him." She pointed at Rodrigo. "After I know you aren't going to try anything else, I'll hear you out."

Rodrigo flashed a smug grin at Gabriella. Luke gritted his teeth and tightened his fingers around the gun.

Gabriella ordered Rodrigo to stand up. She dragged the chair across the room so it sat in the center of the shooting lane and instructed Rodrigo to take a seat. Luke took a stand in front of Rodrigo, the weapon aimed at his chest. Gabriella stepped behind the chair and held up the rope. Her eyes met Luke's briefly. He'd have to remember to thank his brothers for playing so many cops and robbers games, complete with tying each other up.

"Make sure his palms are facing each other as you cinch them together."

She nodded and bent down to get to work. Rodrigo squirmed but said nothing as she tied his hands. A moment later, she stood. "Let's get you patched up," she whispered to Luke.

So that was why she'd moved the chair so far away. She wanted to talk. Gabriella insisted Luke take the leather recliner. The soft padding almost put him to sleep the moment he sat. His leg finally found relief.

"I'm afraid I need you to take the flannel shirt off." She helped yank the sleeve off so he could keep his left arm as straight as possible. The navy shirt underneath was more moist than he realized. He closed his eyes, fighting sleep, but he knew he wouldn't make it if he saw the blood.

The crackle of plastic and paper meant she'd found something to help stop the blood flow. She tugged on the shirt's collar, and he felt her fingers work. "I'm trying to clean you up a little first," she said. "Do you think he's right?"

Luke cracked open one eye. She meant Rodrigo and his prediction that Benito wouldn't let them live anyway. He wanted to soothe the worried lines between her brows but couldn't lie to her. "It's crossed my mind."

She pressed her lips together. "I'm going to apply pressure."

The sudden agony brought colors to his vision. Without the warning, he would've screamed. The pain dropped to an ache. His skin pulled against something sticky. She'd bandaged him tight. "Sorry," she whispered. "I wanted to make sure the bleeding slowed."

He nodded but couldn't speak yet.

"I knew it was a risk but thought… I mean, Aunt Freddie has Alzheimer's, I thought they'd leave her alone." Her voice remained hushed. Rodrigo likely heard her voice but probably couldn't make out her words. "And I don't even know what to make of this whole coin issue."

He coughed and cleared his throat. "If there are really gold coins from the early nineteen hundreds on this property, they'd be worth millions. Coins are hard to reproduce. That's why they hold their value."

"How do you know that?"

"My dad had a coin collection. Nothing big. Started with coins he'd find on the construction site, and then he bought the state quarters."

She pursed her lips. "So if the rest of the mafia finds out about it, they'll never leave us alone." Her mouth parted as her eyes widened. "What if he has a phone? Can you check him?" Gabriella held out a hand.

Luke sighed. So much for the short reprieve. He set down his weapon and accepted her hand. The rocking motion of the recliner helped him up with relatively little additional pain.

Rodrigo stiffened when he saw Luke, likely nervous about retribution. The temptation to punch Rodrigo was strong, but Luke shook it off. If he truly believed the Lord was his defender, then he'd have to let go of the desire to have vengeance. Dust and sand fell on his hand as he rifled through Rodrigo's pockets.

Success! He found a smartphone and a set of keys but not their own keys. "You have a vehicle. Where?"

Rodrigo frowned. "In the foothills."

Gabriella grabbed the phone from his good hand before he got a second look. She held up the cracked screen. "Let's hope it still works." She hit the power button. Luke looked over her shoulder, praying it would power up. A red bar on the top of the screen lit up. Only 10 percent battery left.

"You don't want to do that," Rodrigo said. "We can work out a deal."

"It's almost three o'clock," she muttered. "We don't have much time." Gabriella met Luke's gaze as she clicked the recorder application, then slipped it into her pocket as if she'd turned it off. "Explain the evidence," she said.

Rodrigo rolled his eyes. "The less you know the better, sweetheart. Let's talk deal."

"No deal until I hear exactly what my mother risked everything for. Tell me everything."

Rodrigo shrugged, but he stared into her face. "Your funeral."

For the next ten minutes, Rodrigo rambled on about crime bosses, drug dealings and the murder of Gabriella's grandfather.

Gabriella blinked back tears. "His own brother suggested they put a hit on him?"

"Claudio knew being family only went so far," Rodrigo muttered.

Luke couldn't imagine. Family meant everything to him, but the crime family described it more like a cult. The moment he got out of this, he was taking a long overdue trip to Northern California to see his parents, with a stop in Oregon to visit with David and his new sister-in-law, Aria. His eyes drifted to Gabriella. He'd always hoped he could introduce her to the family as something more than a friend. And for a split second when they kissed, he'd thought it a possibility.

Gabriella questioned Rodrigo further about the evidence spread out on the cabinet. Luke's hands itched to get back to the ledger on top. It wasn't related to the Mirabella family. It was part ledger, part work diary of the sand and mining business. Gabriella would be glad to know her mother seemed to run an aboveboard business—she even filed taxes for the business underneath her pseudonym of Samantha Radcliffe. But after Gabriella's reaction at finding out he'd read the journal, maybe he'd let her discover that tidbit herself.

Gabriella crossed her arms across her chest. "I think you've answered all my questions."

Rodrigo raised an eyebrow. "So you let me go, show me to the coins and I'll take care of Benito. I'll make sure your aunt and yourself get a nice little stipend from the coins and are set for life."

"Why would I believe you over Benito?"

He narrowed his eyes. "I told you. Your uncle trusted me. I know about the coins. That's why." He shrugged. "I'll even let you keep my weapon as a sign of good faith."

Gabriella pulled the phone out of her pocket and turned off the voice recording application. She sighed. "I have a better idea. I give Benito the evidence, don't tell him about the coins and give the authorities this to take care of the whole lot of you." She shook the phone at him.

Rodrigo's face turned beet red, and he burst upright, taking the chair with him. "He'll kill you if I don't beat him to it first!"

Gabriella jerked backward and wrapped herself in her arms. She still shivered.

Luke kicked Rodrigo in the stomach and he fell back,

the chair landing upright but tilted back. "Next time I'm using the gun," Luke growled.

Rodrigo's face contorted as he screamed at Gabriella.

If they had any more rope, he'd tie both of Rodrigo's legs to the chair, but he figured they should be thankful to find any at all. He comforted himself with the fact that it'd be near impossible for Rodrigo to move fast or travel up the stairs with a chair attached to his back.

Gabriella's face paled.

"Are you okay?"

She blinked rapidly and nodded. "Before the battery dies…" She pulled up the email application and attached the voice recording to send to her own email address.

"Good idea," he said.

Her hands shook as she handed him the phone. "Call your mom. Please. If she's anything like you, then I can trust she'll know the right person to call. I should've let you do that in the first place. Rodrigo is right. I'm out of my league."

Luke didn't take the time to argue with her. He'd understood her reasons to wait until now, but not only was time running out, the phone's battery was down to 3 percent. Never before had he been so thankful that his parents had kept a landline. The same phone number he'd memorized as a young man. In fact it was the only phone number he knew by heart. Every other contact was inside his smartphone and computer.

The phone rang two times. *Please don't let it go to voice mail. Please let someone be there, Lord.* It rang once more. After the fourth ring he knew it'd be diverted to the recording.

"Hello." His mother's voice rang through the phone more like an exclamation than a greeting.

"Mom, it's Luke."

"Hi, sweetie. It's good to hear your—"

"I don't have much time. I need you to use your network to find law enforcement you trust in the Treasure Valley. Send them to the Radcliffe Ranch."

Gabriella didn't waste time while he spoke. She stacked and shoved the evidence back into the deposit bag. Luke placed a hand over the ledger as she reached for it. "This one isn't part of the evidence."

She tilted her head.

"You can find out yourself later," he said. "Mom, we're dealing with the Mirabella crime family. They've insinuated they have moles inside the police or FBI. I don't know which."

"What? Luke, don't you dare tease about this." His mother's voice rose an octave. "If you boys keep getting yourselves mixed up with the mafia, you're going to give me a heart attack."

Luke glanced at Gabriella's eager face and thought of her own mother, who did end up having a heart attack. "Ma, I'm serious and don't even joke about that. They're holding my friend Gabriella's great-aunt hostage. The switch is supposed to happen here in—"

The sound of wind chimes filled his ear and then, nothing. He pulled the phone down to take a good look. His shoulders sagged. "The battery died. There's a chance she got enough information to send for help, but now—"

"We're on our own."

FIFTEEN

Gabriella pulled out the strap from the deposit bag, attached it to either end and twisted the key to lock the bag. She slipped the key into the pocket of her jeans. A steely calm settled over her nerves.

Help wasn't on the way because she'd refused to ask for it until too late. If she'd listened to Luke earlier, she might've had more options, but she couldn't see reason until Rodrigo spelled out the truth. Even if she did convince Benito that her great-aunt wasn't a risk, they were likely going to kill her.

But the Mirabella family didn't know about Luke yet, and she intended to keep it that way. "I'm going alone."

He laughed aloud, but his eyes flashed with frustration. "If you say that one more time, Gabriella…"

"I'm not trying to be a martyr here, Luke. I have a plan to stall them until help arrives. I'll turn the tables on them. I let them know I have Rodrigo. That he plans to be a witness."

"Keep me out of it," Rodrigo shouted. She ignored the threats he unleashed yet again.

"So you want me to stay here," Luke stated. "Not going to happen."

"To stay with Rodrigo." She gestured at the weapon on the top of the counter. "I imagine his gun alone will tie the family to some more crimes."

He gritted his teeth and took a step closer to her. The intensity in his gaze made her breath catch. "For me it was never a rebound, Gabriella." He shook his head. "I was totally head over heels in love with you." He looked at the ceiling. "But too immature to handle rejection." His eyes met her gaze. "Even though that wasn't your intention. I understand that now. But seeing you again… you haven't changed. You're the best friend I haven't seen in years. My heart missed you, Gabriella, and if you think I'm going to let you walk through that door alone when you might not come…" He swallowed and shook his head. "We go together or not at all."

She pressed a hand over her mouth and closed her eyes, willing her throat to stop throbbing with every beat of her heart so she could speak again. He'd loved her? He had been her best friend, and no one had ever matched the friendship they'd developed…

If she was honest with herself, her heart missed him, too, but could she really say that she loved him with everything going on? What if it was all adrenaline induced? What if he changed his mind and moved on, leaving her to take years to recover again? If they got out of this, there would be so much to sort through before her life calmed down. Could he really be there for all of that? After her name would likely be dragged in the mud?

"I just want you to hear me, Gabriella. I'm not expecting you to say anything. My timing, as usual, probably stinks."

She opened her eyes and her chest warmed. It was

exactly what she needed him to say. Another exhale helped her focus. "I love my great-aunt, and I have to at least try."

He raised an eyebrow, but his blue eyes never strayed. "So let's go."

"And Rodrigo?"

"Look at him. He can't go anywhere. And even if he made it around the room, he'd never be able to get up those stairs."

It was true that Luke helped her keep a level head, and he didn't look ready to back down. Had he really meant that? Was he really in love with her? She reached for his right hand. Luke wrapped his fingers around her hand. "Okay. Let's go," she said. "The clock is ticking. We have less than an hour to get across the property, and we don't even know the weather and…"

He moved her hand to his heart and bowed his head. "Be with us, Lord." His eyes flashed open. "Now, we go."

The pain of constantly tense muscles vanished. She inhaled. "Together."

"Help me move the mini fridge?"

She didn't understand what he meant until she helped haul it to the bottom step. Luke closed the door and then kicked the fridge so it leaned against the door to block it. "A precautionary measure."

Her heartbeat reminded her of a ticking clock. Time moved too fast. There were several miles to cover to get back to the front gate. And depending on the weather, they'd never get there fast enough. Rodrigo said he had a vehicle in the foothills, but that again would take too long to reach. Besides, as soon as he knew her intentions, she couldn't trust a word out of his mouth. Not that he had been truthful anyway.

They crossed the wooden floor, and Gabriella shoved the barn door open. The rainfall had diminished to a drizzle, but the air smelled dirty, like a wet dog who sat too close to a campfire.

"This isn't going to be a fun hike," Luke remarked.

Gabriella threw the strap diagonally over her torso. She had put her mother's and Rodrigo's guns in the deposit bag with the rest of the evidence. It had to weigh at least thirty pounds, and her shoulder already smarted with the pressure. Luke carried the other guns. One thing was for sure: neither of them would be able to run.

Her mind made up, she turned due south.

"This is the fastest way?"

She cringed, knowing she'd be testing their friendship. But it was the only way. "It will be," she acknowledged.

Every step kicked up dust around her ankles. They passed the final corner of the barn. She spotted the stable in the distance, a little way up the hillside. Luke staggered to a stop. "Wait a minute." He gave her a questioning look.

She worried her lip. "Sorry."

He groaned and dropped his head. "Horses. Why'd it have to be horses?"

"I'll take care of everything. They'll come to me. I'll saddle them. You don't have to get near them."

"Until we need to ride them."

She shrugged. "Or you could…"

He held up a hand. "Don't even start that again." He shook his head and trudged forward. "Horses," he muttered.

"I hope they're okay. They're able to access the stables at all times but even in storms, sometimes they favor standing together in the pasture rather than coming in. I'm worried about them. If they inhaled all the dust…"

"Then they won't be very speedy," Luke finished.

She flicked open the latch on the front of the stable door. Inside there was a long row of stalls, but only two of them had the back end open. There was some dust on the floor, but thankfully nothing like she imagined. She opened the gate to the two stalls in question and walked past the water and grain bucket. The water would need to be changed immediately. She pointed to the hose hanging over a beam. "Are you up for it?"

"Pretty sure I can do that one-handed. Why don't these two stalls have a divide between them?"

"Horses are social. Ours don't like to be separated."

Gabriella walked through the stable and into the second hallway behind the stable—the one that led to the open pasture. Here the dust and sand looked to be almost an inch thick. But there were hoofprints leading up to the stables and back out.

"Good news. I think they sought out shelter during the storm." She reentered the stable and ducked her fingers underneath the stream of water out of the hose. "I hope they still come when I call. I haven't done this in ages." She flung the water off her hands and stepped back into the hallway.

Unfortunately, Luke stared right at her. She turned away slightly. She'd never had an audience before, and what she was about to do was a bit…odd. Gabriella tucked her lips underneath her teeth, stuck her index fingers inside her mouth and released a high-pitched, loud whistle.

"I can't believe you."

Gabriella turned to the sound of Luke's voice, her cheeks flaming. "I know…it's a little unladylike, but it works."

He frowned. "You've known how to do that all this time and never taught me? I've *always* wanted to be able to whistle like that."

Gabriella laughed. Luke never ceased to surprise her. Was there anything he wouldn't accept about her? Her face fell at the thought. She really was falling for him, wasn't she? She gritted her teeth and inhaled. If she softened now she wouldn't be able to do what was necessary to save her aunt. "Maybe I'll show you sometime."

His eyes glinted. "My brothers will be jealous."

A soft neigh and the sound of hooves approaching echoed against the cement walls as two magnificent animals entered the long hallway. "There are my ladies. You want some hay?"

They knew that word. They quickened their pace toward her. Gabriella flicked her hand. "Get out of sight, Luke. They don't know you."

Her gaze drifted to the bale of hay. Dust in hay meant dust inside the horses' lungs. "This won't do." She picked up the bale and carried it past the gate. She closed the gates and talked in hushed tones. "Let me get the hay, ladies."

They stuck their muzzles in the space over the gate, as if waiting to see a show. Gabriella strode past the other stalls to get to the gargantuan pile of hay bales. Luke stood in the third stall. "Is this really necessary?" he whispered. "Or are you doing it for my sake?"

She shrugged. "Does it have to be one or the other?"

Even the light banter drove her crazy. They should be at the front of the gate by now. She hurriedly grabbed the first couple of hay bales and threw them behind her. Hopefully the bales more toward the center would have less dust. Something buzzed past her, but she didn't hesitate to grab the next bale and then...

Gabriella froze. Bees buzzed past her head.

"Don't move," Luke said behind her. "Looks like they thought they found a good place to gather during the storm."

Acknowledging him would mean opening her mouth, and she wasn't about to do that. More buzzing around her. Had they built a hive somewhere in the stable walls? Or worse, at the back of the hay bales?

She took a step backward. One buzzed into her hair. She flinched and an uncontrollable screech escaped. A sharp sting on the side of her neck. She slapped the side of her face, arms flailing, and ran down the hall until the buzzing stopped.

Luke ran to her, his face pale. "Did you?"

She lifted her chin. *Please let him say it was my imagination.*

"Stay still." Luke's fingers grazed the area just underneath her chin. A small scratch and then he straightened. "I think I got the stinger out."

Gabriella rubbed her forehead. Her eyes burned. Whether it was psychological or not, her face already itched. "We can't win." Her voice sounded as pitiful as she felt. How could she save her aunt when her body would start attacking itself?

Luke's stomach twisted. He exhaled forcefully after realizing he'd been holding his breath. A look over his shoulder confirmed the bees were still buzzing around the hay bales, but they were leaving them alone farther down the hallway.

Gabriella scratched her face.

His heart lurched to his throat. "It's starting? Can you still breathe?"

She nodded and tears ran down her cheek. "It doesn't happen immediately. At least it didn't last time."

"How soon?"

"I don't know." She sniffed and ran her fingertips underneath her eyes to stop the tears. "Soon."

"The EpiPen. You said you had one in the glove compartment of your car."

The area just below her chin turned into a red circle. Her lips seemed puffier than they had a second ago. Was it his imagination? He racked his brain. His friend from junior high had a bee allergy. What had he said? That they should move the least amount possible so the bee venom doesn't spread as fast.

"Stay here."

"But…"

He held up a finger. "Don't talk. Stay still." He strode to the gate and flung it open. Mercifully, the horses didn't run. But to ensure that at least one of them would stay put he'd need to step behind them and close the back exit. His scalp tingled, and his breathing grew shallow. He could do this. He just needed to make sure he didn't spook them.

Luke lifted his shaking right hand and let the horse on the right smell him. She eyed him and lifted her head slightly as if she was saying, "Whoa. What happened to you?"

"It's been a bad day," Luke said in hushed tones.

"And I could really use your help not making it an even worse one." He glided his hand up her neck and across the side, so the horse would know where he was at all times. "So, if you could please not kick me in the head, that'd be great."

He froze at the back flank. The horse whipped her tail, seemingly annoyed.

Luke closed his eyes and took another step. So far so good. He opened his eyes and gently pulled the back door closed. He took a giant step until he was back at the flank and realized he'd been holding his breath. "Thank you," he exhaled.

He grabbed the saddle with his right hand. He'd need to make quick work of it, but that'd be difficult—almost impossible—with only one good arm to do the job. The horse stepped slightly to the side. Luke jerked and spun around. Gabriella's face looked splotchy, and her forehead was creased.

"What are you doing? I told you to stay put."

"If you want to save me in time, you'll need help." She slipped on the bit underneath the horse's tongue and flicked up the reins over its ears.

Luke strained his back as he flung the saddle on top of the horse. "Sorry," he muttered to the mare. "But if you help, the venom will take hold faster—"

Gabriella grabbed her throat with both hands, her eyes wide. "It's so itchy."

They were running out of time. He groaned as he enlisted the help of his other arm. The searing pain of the movement almost sent him to his knees. Hot moisture seeped through the bandage and into his shirt, but he'd rather die fighting to save Gabriella than lose her when he hadn't given it his all. He latched the saddle, kicked the water bucket over and used it as a stepping stool.

Luke mounted the horse and situated himself as far back as possible. He reached for Gabriella with his good arm. She pressed off the bucket and mounted just in front of him. With slight pressure from his left heel, he guided the horse closer to the gate. As soon as they were into the front hallway he shoved the gate closed to keep the other horse from running free.

"Hang on," he whispered, gave the mare a light kick and launched into motion.

They ducked as they ran through the front stable entry into the open. Luke wrapped his arm around Gabriella to help her balance and kept the reins in his right hand. She said nothing but pointed in the northeast direction.

His fist clenched the reins. If she pointed without talking did that mean her throat was closing? Luke pressed his right knee into the horse, leading its canter in the right direction. The movement and the struggle to align his hip movements with the horse's movements pulled at his other wound.

The dizzy sensation returned. *Help me stay conscious, Lord. I need Your help.* If he were a lighter man he'd no doubt have passed out by now. He had all those double cheeseburgers and weight-lifting sessions to thank for his mass and the fact that he could probably stand to lose more blood than the average fellow.

They passed the alfalfa fields and weaved between trees. The lake was in sight now. He guided the horse on the grass, as close to the beach as possible. If they stayed on this course, then…there! He could see the house.

Luke leaned forward slightly, pushing the horse to

go faster. Gabriella jostled in his arms for a moment, then drooped. "No, no, no. Hang on. Hang on, Gabriella!" She didn't move or respond.

The horse slowed to a trot until Luke pressed his leg into its side again. "We need to help her!"

All the pain from his wounds disappeared from his awareness. The only sensation—lava in his core—remained. He rode past the shed, the shovel on the ground... "Faster!" They rounded the corner of the house and onto the driveway. The horse trotted to the side of his truck. Luke jumped off the horse onto the top of his truck, dragging Gabriella with him, tucking her within the safety of his arms. His back hit the roof, but he moved before the pain could set.

He slid Gabriella off his torso and onto the hood of his car. Her face was a sickly shade of purple, her lips swollen, her neck covered in splotches. "I can't lose you. Gabriella, hang on!"

Luke sprinted to her car. He dove for the largest rock he could see near the lake's edge and smashed it into the passenger side window of her car. The glass shattered, sprinkling all around his feet. The car alarm pierced the still air around him.

He reached past the jagged remaining shards to the glove compartment. He pulled up the lever and felt it give way. "Be there, be there..."

Underneath an auto manual and the car registration he spied the corner of a green box. He grabbed it and ran to the hood of his truck as he opened the box. He yanked out the first injector, flicked off the yellow lid and stabbed the pen into the side of her thigh.

His own breathing ragged, he watched her face. "Please...breathe..."

She didn't move, she didn't flinch. "Come on…" He pressed the area that he'd injected, hoping that'd help the medicine absorb faster into her body. Though he had no idea if that would do any good.

Still nothing. He shifted her body closer to the edge of the hood, ready to start CPR. He reached for her wrist and pressed his fingertips. *Lord, please save her. Please!* Only twenty-four hours ago he'd felt her strong heartbeat and now…

What was that? He let go and repositioned his fingers an inch above her wrist, next to her thumb. A light pulse. He exhaled. He watched her mouth, parted. Her chest didn't rise and fall, though. Was her throat still so swollen she couldn't breathe?

Luke leaned over to start mouth-to-mouth. He cupped his right hand underneath her neck and used his left to tilt her chin up slightly.

Gabriella gasped. Her hands flung to her throat. Her eyes flashed open and stared into his. Her car alarm reached its automatic shutoff time. Only the sound of water sloshing the banks and the leaves shifting in the breeze remained.

Luke jerked back. His breath sounded like a garbled laugh. "You're alive."

She nodded, but her whole body convulsed. He pulled her whole body into his arms, close to his chest, and dropped his head over her, his face touching her hair as she continued to shiver. He blinked against his blurry vision. "I need to get you to a hospital. I almost lost you."

"Benadryl," she whispered.

He straightened and sat her up on the hood. "Where?"

She pointed at her car. Luke held her shoulders for

a brief second, making sure she was stable, and darted back. Nothing in the glove compartment...the center console! He found a pill bottle and cracked it open as he ran back to her. A few pills flew out of the bottle and to the ground from his jerky movements.

She flipped her palm over and Luke shook fifteen into her hand. She said nothing but grabbed two of the tablets and chewed them, flinching as she did. "Tastes horrible."

Water. She needed water. Luke ran back to the bank and grabbed another rock. He crossed the small space to his truck.

Gabriella's eyes widened. "What are you—"

He turned his head, closed his eyes and slammed the rock into his own car window. The shattering glass pricked the top of his hand as the siren's repetitive wail filled the air. He flicked the window fragment off his hand, hauled himself up onto the running board and reached into the back of the cab to grab three water bottles with his right hand.

Gabriella's soft eyes followed his every movement as he presented the water to her. She accepted one with a shy smile, closed her eyes and lifted the bottle. Her left hand rubbed her throat downward as she sipped. She set the bottle down and inhaled. "Thank you," she mouthed.

He didn't blame her for not shouting over the wails. Two minutes seemed like a lifetime to wait until his own alarm shut off. Thankfully the vehicles were relatively new, so they were set up not to last long enough to negatively impact the batteries.

Luke exhaled a sigh of relief as the car stopped wailing. "Still hurts?" He gestured to her throat.

She shivered and nodded.

Luke placed his hands over her arms, ready to pick her up again. "Are you cold?"

"No. It's the pen. Makes me shaky and hot for a while. It means the medicine is working." She took another sip. "And the allergy medicine I swallowed should help prevent a repeat. Until I can get to a hospital."

"I'll get the horse."

SIXTEEN

Gabriella reached out a hand and placed it on his chest. "No. What time is it?"

Luke's face fell. "I should've known." He stepped back to his car and leaned into it. "The car says it's quarter 'til four."

Fifteen minutes until their time was up. Her head throbbed, making it hard to concentrate. "Well, hopefully help will be coming soon." She gestured to both cars. "You sure tried to alert anyone in hearing distance."

He raised an eyebrow as he approached and suddenly he was right in front of her. "Not ready to laugh about it yet."

She searched his darkened eyes. He'd faced his fear for her. He risked his own safety to rescue her. He'd stayed with her, in harm's way, despite many chances to leave her on her own. Luke would never treat her heart carelessly. How could she have ever imagined differently?

Fear. She didn't want to hurt anymore. Every bone in her body felt full of cement, every muscle ached, her throat stung, but it wasn't that type of pain she feared.

She reached out absentmindedly to his chest, to his own heart.

Uncertainty flickered across his face as his gaze moved to her hand. But now wasn't the time. Time... "We have to head for the gate," she said, pulling her fingers back.

His shoulders dropped, but he didn't argue. "What did you have in mind?"

She unzipped the bag and pulled out Rodrigo's gun. "I need you to hold onto this."

He raised an eyebrow but accepted it. "I set the other guns down in the stables."

That was news to her. Gabriella really didn't want him to have to use it for protection, but it was better than nothing. "We need to walk down closer to the gate. The trees get pretty thick on the north side." She pulled out her mother's gun and tucked it behind her. Except if they searched her and found her armed it might make things take a turn for the worse. She couldn't risk her aunt.

"Take this one, too," Gabriella said and handed it to him.

Luke frowned. "I don't understand."

"I'm hoping you will keep an eye on me."

He scoffed. "I'm going with you."

"Yes. And then you're going to hide."

Luke's forehead creased.

"You have a family," Gabriella pleaded. "The last thing I want is for them to have more leverage. If they find out about you, if they know you're a witness, then they might seek out your parents, your brothers..."

Luke held up a hand. "I get it. I don't like it, but I get it."

"And if things don't go as planned—"

"Then I'll do my best to have good aim."

A soft laugh escaped past her lips. "Let's pray we don't have to go that far." She jutted her chin forward. "We need to hurry."

Luke hobbled forward. The strain it must have put on his injuries to ride her to safety, to save her. Gabriella couldn't imagine the amount of suffering he was enduring. She adjusted the deposit bag so it rested on her left hip. She stepped to his left side and lifted his arm gingerly.

He glanced down and rested his injured arm around her shoulder. Gabriella slipped her arm around the back of his waist. "Lean on me so your hip doesn't have to strain so much."

Luke sighed. "We don't need to put any added strain on you, either."

"We're quite a pair," she admitted, pushing forward. "At least I have the extra EpiPen with me, just in case."

"I think I have a new fear of bees, as well," Luke admitted.

An involuntary shiver coursed down her spine.

"Sorry," Luke said. "That was insensitive of me. Are you okay?"

"Mmm-hmm. Let's just keep moving." Gabriella led him into the line of trees. The two-mile roundabout driveway's center point was the house. She figured they had at least three-quarters of a mile to go before she got to the gate.

Her view drifted to across the asphalt. The lake glistened with the reflection of the sun bursting through the gray clouds. Her thoughts rested on her aunt. Would Benito make good on the deal and let her walk away?

Tears pricked her eyes. She squeezed Luke closer.

She hated to lose him so soon after finding him, but in her heart, Gabriella knew she would do whatever it took to stand between Benito and her aunt.

"What are you thinking about?" Luke asked.

"Possibilities," Gabriella whispered.

"Whatsoever things are true, whatsoever things are honest, whatsoever things are just, whatsoever things are pure, whatsoever things are lovely…"

Gabriella tilted her head up to find him looking down at her. "I'm thinking about one who is all those things."

Luke stopped. "Gabriella…"

She rose up on her toes and kissed his cheek, relishing the comforting touch of his hand on her back, even the stubble on his face against hers. "I never would've gotten this far without you," she whispered. She stepped away from him. "I think you should hide now."

His jaw firmed and as she took another step away, he reached for her hand. Their gazes stayed locked on each other for the briefest of moments. He closed his eyes. "Lord, help us, please."

After a lifetime of growing up in church and attending a Christian college, it was probably the simplest yet most heartfelt prayer she'd heard. She squeezed his right hand in response, then left him in the forested area. The moment her feet hit the asphalt she felt exposed despite the fact Luke stood guard, watching. The sound of twigs, and birds and crickets… The skin on the back of her neck tingled. The air seemed to crackle with electricity.

Only a few more feet, and she would be at the electronic gate. To her left, gargantuan boulders stood. The one in front had the name of the ranch engraved, but it stood as a reminder: focus on the rock, her Lord, her

Savior, the most honest, the most true and pure thing she could think on.

Two black vehicles pulled up on the side of the road, parallel to the gate. Gabriella's heart sped into overdrive. She forced her lungs to take slow, rhythmic breaths, but a dizzy sensation passed. She stumbled and reached for the control box. The metal lid scraped against the rest of the box, setting her teeth on edge. Whoever sat in the darkened windows of the sedan could see her, could shoot her at any moment.

Whatsoever things are true...

Gabriella typed the access code into the keypad and heard the telltale click of whirring motors. She stepped back as the gate swung open. The sedans backed up at a diagonal, as if ready to pull into the driveway.

Gabriella turned on her heel, trying not to seem eager, but she needed to be in front of the vehicles so that Luke would be able to see her. If she walked just a little further, the driveway was at enough of a curve no one would be able to see them from the road.

She speed walked without the telltale arms at a ninety-degree angle. Her legs tightened and sped forward. She stepped into the middle of the driveway and held a hand up. The sedans angled and parked in a V shape.

The passenger doors on the right sedan and left sedan opened at the same time. The same slick-dressed men in suits stepped out—Benito on the right and the one who would give her nightmares on the left. Benito nodded to the bag on her hip. "I hope that's what I need."

"It is," she said. "And I have even more to offer," she added. Gabriella tilted her chin up. "As long as we reach an agreement."

Benito placed his hands together and raised them up until his fingertips were just underneath his chin. He laughed a hollow chuckle. "Is that so? I knew you were Renata's girl through and through the moment I saw you." He dropped his hands and shrugged, as if he were just humoring her. "What you got for me?"

"First, my aunt."

"Take off the bag and show me you're not carrying."

Gabriella hated taking the bag off her person, but she lifted it over her head, lifted her shirt just enough to show her waistband and spun around. Benito nodded at the man to the left.

He opened the passenger car door. Slumped in the seat in the blue quilted bathrobe Gabriella had given her for Christmas, Aunt Freddie lifted her chin slightly. Her eyes met Gabriella's, and she straightened. Good. That meant Aunt Freddie understood what was going on.

"She's no threat to you," Gabriella called out. "I told you, she has dementia. Let her go."

Aunt Freddie looked up at the ceiling of the car and around, a bit dramatic for Gabriella's taste, but that meant Freddie understood and would act the part. If only Aunt Freddie didn't actually struggle with dementia, but at least she had her lucid moments, like now.

The gunman left the door open but stood in front of her aunt, blocking her view.

"So what else you have for me?"

Gabriella shook her head. "No. I give you the evidence, and you give me my aunt before we discuss further."

Luke strained his ears from his hiding place behind a mature oak tree. One of the thugs turned his way, and

Luke tucked his head behind the bark. No shouts, no gunfire…hopefully he hadn't blown it for Gabriella. He looked down at his feet, careful where to step as he peeked around the opposite side of the tree. From this vantage point he couldn't see what was happening as well. He could see the backside of Gabriella's head, but that was it. How was he supposed to keep her safe without getting a visual on the gunmen?

Twigs crackled up ahead. Luke strained his ears and squinted into the shaded woods. A large animal…deer? No, horse. That's where she went after his truck's siren had gone off. Another animal trotted up. Two?

Dread built in his stomach. The second horse had followed. But how? Luke replayed the events in the stable over in his mind. His adrenaline had been at an all-time high, but he distinctly recalled closing the back gate and front gate. The second horse would've had no way to get out unless…

Luke leaned forward. One of the horses also had a saddle and the reins…were tied to a tree! So the one that trotted up had to be the horse they had ridden, but the one tied to the tree…

Luke looked around, frantic. There, across the driveway, at the bend, hiding among the boulders along the lake. Rodrigo crouched down, a weapon in his hands and a murderous look in his eyes. He advanced slowly, methodically along the lake, heading toward the gate… and his eyes weren't set on the car. He planned to murder Gabriella before she could give Rodrigo up…or the existence of the treasury coin stash. And there went any chance of Gabriella using Rodrigo to guarantee the mafia left the property without killing Gabriella and Aunt Freddie.

Luke had never before wished that he and his brothers had more shooting practice than the unofficial nail-gun contests they'd rig up on their dad's construction sites. *I need good aim, Lord. Don't let him get her.*

Rodrigo crept closer. Any second and he'd have his target. Luke pulled out the gun from his waistband and lifted it. Rodrigo darted behind a boulder the size of a small car. Had he seen Luke? Or was he hiding from one of the mafia men?

Luke wanted to call out to Gabriella. He couldn't see Rodrigo anymore. For all he knew, Rodrigo was taking aim at her right now.

Luke slipped around the tree to where he'd almost been discovered. It couldn't be helped—he had to have a better view. Rodrigo's shoulder poked between two of the boulders, then dipped down again.

Luke studied the trajectory of where he imagined Rodrigo lay. Rodrigo would be able to shoot Gabriella. If not there, then in a foot or two, and Luke had no way to get a clean shot.

His right leg gave slightly. He steadied himself against the bark and fought off the lightheadedness. Only one option presented itself, but it would require speed and most of all courage and strength that he didn't feel. *Lord, help me.*

Luke shoved the gun back in its place, tightened his left fist and hit the tree. It hurt enough to spike his adrenaline. Before he could second-guess himself, before it was too late, Luke left his hiding place and hurdled over the fern in front of him. His shoes hit the moss and slipped slightly.

"Hey!"

Luke disregarded the voices yelling and launched

himself to the asphalt before he lost all balance. He pumped his arms, running at a sprint. Gabriella spun around, her long brown hair cascading around her in an arc, her brown eyes wide. Her mouth parted open in horror.

"Rodrigo," he shouted. Luke pointed to the boulders with his left hand as he made the gesture to get down with his right arm.

Gabriella ducked as the crack of a bullet split the air. "Get down, Aunt Freddie," she screamed as she cradled the top of her head with her arms. Awareness crossed Benito's features but morphed into rage.

"Get him," Benito yelled. The drivers' doors opened, and two more gunmen jumped out of the sedans, their weapons aimed at the boulders. Rodrigo popped up and fired off a couple of rounds. One driver fell back. The other howled, shot in the shoulder. The gunman in front of Freddie steeled his aim, and Rodrigo ducked back underneath the boulder.

"Give it up, Rodrigo. You will never be in charge." Benito also had his gun aimed at the boulder.

Rodrigo jumped up again, except his gun pointed directly at Gabriella. Luke dove in front of her as gunfire crackled all around him.

"No," Gabriella cried as he fell against her.

And then silence. No more gunfire. Luke rolled onto his back, onto the asphalt, and instinctively reached for his aching shoulder, which was bleeding more than before. Pain registered all over his body, but was it worse than before? He hadn't felt the telltale ripping of flesh like the other two times. Was it possible he wasn't hit?

The man who'd been in front of her aunt crouched down and approached the boulder just past them. He looked back at Benito, ignoring Gabriella and Luke. "I got him, boss."

Tears welled in Gabriella's eyes as she hunched over him. "Are you okay? Please be okay."

Luke's throat tightened. *What do we do now, Lord?* Their only chance of being able to walk away from the mafia had just been killed.

Luke also proved no use to Gabriella. He couldn't shoot off the gunmen one by one. He was no match against them, especially with his other shoulder throbbing from the impact of the asphalt. The muscles around that shoulder went into spasms. He tried to move his arm, and severe pain rushed past his upper back to his spine. Luke knew that feeling. He'd had it once before after a particularly intense "dogpile" with his brothers—he'd dislocated his shoulder.

"Luke, talk to me," Gabriella cried.

The gunman who investigated Rodrigo shook his head in disgust and walked past them to the sedan. Luke cried out through the pain and moved his right hand to his waistband. "Gabriella," he whispered.

Her eyes widened and she leaned forward. He pulled the gun from its hiding place and slipped it into her waiting hands. Her face paled.

"You have to be okay," she said.

"Cry more," he whispered.

Her eyes widened for half a second before she understood what he was asking. "Luke," she wailed. She moaned and when she moved her shoulders as if crying, she took the gun from his hand.

She would never make Broadway, but he hoped it would do the job. She attempted to hide the gun in the front of her own waistband. It slipped from her grasp and slammed into his torso. The weight rushed all the air from his lungs and his heels lifted off the ground. "Oof."

"Luke," she cried. Gabriella curled over him, this time genuinely distressed. "I'm so sorry," she whispered. She grabbed the gun and tucked it underneath the hem of her shirt.

"Enough," Benito said. "You can't save him now. Throw over the bag."

Luke exhaled. So at least they thought he'd been shot. The second gun poking into his back started to register over the pain in his shoulders and hip. Benito's little statement proved the men would make sure Luke's heart had stopped beating before they left the property.

SEVENTEEN

Gabriella placed two hands over her stomach—where the gun resided now—as she stood. Her shoulders hunched, she turned, bent over and lifted the canvas bag from the ground. "Who wants it?" she asked. Her voice cracked at the end of the question.

What were her options? What little plan she'd formed in her mind had been ruined. Rodrigo was dead. She had nothing to offer Benito to keep them alive. Except the coins...though she had no idea where Mom had stashed them and no one to corroborate they even existed.

Benito pointed a thumb to the gunman who'd resumed his stance in front of the passenger door where her aunt waited. Gabriella gripped the handle of the canvas bag. She could hurl it as hard as possible and hope it knocked or at least stunned the gunman enough. But Benito still held a gun, and if she threw it too far...

Gabriella stiffened. A slight movement and light streamed in between the gunman and the sedan. Was her aunt sneaking out the other side of the car? The driver had been shot, so maybe her aunt took the chance to run away and hide?

"Here," she said. She took two steps forward, willing the gunman to keep eyes on her. Gabriella reached her arm out as far as her strength would allow. The bag's weight strained her bicep and shoulder. "Take it," she said again. *Please keep Benito's eyes on me, too, Lord.*

The gunman crossed the distance. His fingers lingered on her wrist for a second. Acid rose up her throat until his touch disappeared, taking the bag with him. Blue... The robe was still in the passenger seat, but her aunt had gone out the other side. *Help her run, Lord. Give her strength and wit to hide. Keep her mind clear.*

"It's all there," Gabriella blurted. She needed to keep their eyes on her for as long as possible. If he turned around...

"Leo. Check it," Benito ordered.

The gunman dipped his hand and unzipped the bag. He rifled around the bag for a few minutes. "There's a lot here. Audio cassettes, photographs, a ledger...want me to look for anything in particular?"

"No, that sounds about right. You make any copies?"

She didn't hesitate to answer. "With your guy Rodrigo here? No. I barely made it here in time."

"Rodrigo stopped being my guy the moment he tried to take my rightful place." He raised an eyebrow. "Let me guess. You wanted to offer Rodrigo to me."

Her insides squirmed. She didn't want to mention her aunt again lest they notice her absence. "There may be more to it," she said.

Benito held his hands out, shrugging with the gun in his hand as if it were simply a decoration. "Let me make this crystal clear. Your aunt's chart may have mentioned something about dementia, so I might be willing to let her go, but the only way you're walking away from here, sweetheart, is by agreeing to work with me." His eyes pierced her. "On a probationary basis."

In other words, she'd be worse off than the messed-up family system her mother grew up in. Benito's sidekick zipped up the bag and sent her a wink. Gabriella's lip curled in disgust.

"She's not going anywhere." Her aunt's voice wobbled.

The gunman turned toward the voice. Her great-aunt held a gun, her shoulders covered by a floral nightgown barely visible over the black sedan. Gabriella's mouth dropped. Aunt Freddie must have taken the gun from the deceased driver.

"Keep moving, Leo, and I blow off your head," her aunt hollered.

Benito spun, gun in hand, toward her aunt. Gabriella regained her senses and yanked her gun from its hiding place. "Freeze, Benito!"

His eyes narrowed. The same disbelief Rodrigo initially showed her demonstrated on his face. "One thing my mom did teach me was how to shoot. If you knew her as you claimed, you know she took that very seriously."

The gun Benito trained on her aunt lowered slightly. His eyes darted to Leo.

"Don't even think about it," Luke said, his voice strong. "Drop it. Now."

Gabriella dared a look out of her peripheral vision. Luke had flipped over on his stomach and was propped up on his elbows with a gun aimed at Leo, as well. "You heard the man," she said, her voice as strong and sure as her heart.

Leo narrowed his eyes.

"Nice and slow," Gabriella warned.

Leo raised his hands up in the air and dropped the gun.

"You should be ashamed of yourself," her aunt hollered. "I changed your diapers, young man."

Benito ground his teeth together. "You don't go against the family, Amalia. You knew the consequences."

"That's not my name anymore. Have some respect," her aunt snapped.

Gabriella almost laughed at her aunt's reaction. Freddie had always been a force to be reckoned with as she grew up, but lately, ever since Mom had died, she'd become fragile. She spoke rarely and, since battling the early stages of dementia, the times she did speak rarely made sense.

Gabriella's eyes widened. Although, hadn't Freddie once called Gabriella, Renata? Her mom's real name… She blinked back the sudden hot tears as pieces clicked in place. The combination of exhaustion, adrenaline and shock hit at once. Her hand started to shake. "Just leave," she said. Her voice no longer sounded strong but more like a plea.

Leo dove for her gun.

A gun went off. Gabriella couldn't see who shot, but she hadn't pulled the trigger. Leo wrestled to pull her arm back. She struggled against his pull, turning herself away, yanking her arm back. Agony ripped through the muscles of her shoulder and chest, but she refused to let him pry the gun from her hand.

She attempted to step on his foot, but Leo jumped back. He shoved her. Gabriella's knee gave way, and she crashed to the asphalt. The impact sent a stinging sensation up her bones, and she cried out.

Leo's hands moved to her neck. The sudden pain and lack of oxygen almost blinded her. She thrashed against him, and the grip on her gun loosened.

A fist soared above her forehead and straight into Leo's jaw.

Leo's fingers flew away from her throat. She dropped the gun and held her neck. Every breath hurt like sandpaper stuck inside her throat.

Leo popped off the ground and punched Luke in the stomach. Benito writhed on the ground, holding his chest with his left hand. Aunt Freddie's face looked ashen. She was staring at the gun she'd once held firmly, confused. Oh, no.

Leo fought for Luke's gun.

Gabriella raised her own gun in the air and shot it three times. "Stop," she cried.

The sound of squealing tires hit her before she spotted the source—a police cruiser ramped up the driveway. Gabriella's stomach quivered. The question was who were they here to help? The mafia or her?

Two police officers jumped out of the vehicle. "Freeze. Drop your weapons." A second police cruiser screeched to a stop beside it. A dark blue Dodge Charger parked behind them both. Two men in suits jumped out. "FBI."

Gabriella let the gun fall from her fingertips. She closed her eyes in relief. "Thank you," she whispered. Running footsteps approached. She opened her eyes in time to see the officers taking aim at Benito and Leo.

"Which one of you called the police?" an officer shouted.

Gabriella looked around, as if almost expecting someone to raise a hand. Someone had called the police? Her gaze drifted to her aunt, who was handing the gun to an officer. "Did I kill someone?" she asked, her voice shaking. Her eyes had the lost look.

Her chest tightened. Oh, no. "No, no, she didn't," Gabriella called out. "You saved me, Aunt Freddie." The officer closest frowned. "I think she's the one that called the police," Gabriella explained. "Check the phone from the man closest to her. My aunt struggles with dementia but was lucid when she got his gun. She saved me from being shot. Please be gentle."

The men in the suits walked around the car. "We got a tip from a Mrs. McGuire?"

Luke raised a hand. "That's my mom," he groaned. Luke turned to Gabriella. "You going to be okay?"

She nodded. "More than okay."

A half smile crossed his pale face as his eyes rolled back, and he dropped to the ground. His body crumpled against the asphalt, his head bouncing slightly up after impact.

"No," she cried out. She launched herself to his side on her hands and knees. The officer leaned down and tried to grab her arm. Gabriella flung his hand away from her. "No, please. You have to help him."

She reached for Luke and picked up his head. Hot liquid met her touch. His hands were limp at his side. The angry red area around his shoulder spread, and a line of red streaked down the side of his jeans. Her head lightened at the sight. She sat down fully, careful to lay Luke's head down softly. Her mouth tasted salty as tears ran freely.

She looked up at the officer. "He needs an ambulance. He's lost so much blood."

"Ma'am, we called one the moment we got here," the officer replied.

His partner shoved Leo, bound in handcuffs, past the sedans to the police car. Benito leaned up against the tire of the black sedan, holding his shoulder, while one of the suits drilled him with questions and tapped on what appeared to be Benito's smartphone.

The wail of sirens approaching confirmed the officer's statement. Gabriella grabbed Luke's right hand and squeezed it. "You stay with me, Luke McGuire. You're not about to get out of this friendship so easily this time."

The screech of brakes and the abrupt end of the sirens meant the paramedics had arrived. Gabriella kept her eyes locked on Luke's face. She leaned over and kissed his cheek. "I love you," she whispered.

The words rushed warmth up her spine. Her heart beat faster. Saying the words aloud somehow made it feel even stronger in her core. It was true. She loved this man deeply.

A female wearing a navy pullover with a paramedic logo stooped in front of her. "Ma'am, I'm with Treasure Valley Paramedics. I'm going to assess your injuries now, okay?"

Gabriella shook her head. "No, take care of him."

"They are, ma'am. I'm here for you."

She blinked and noticed two men preparing to lift Luke onto a stretcher. They counted and lifted at the same time. Luke's fingers slipped from her grasp. *Please don't let it be forever, Lord.*

* * *

Something pulled on his skin, stinging. Luke blinked. The sight of white walls and a stranger hovering over him jarred him awake.

"Mr. McGuire," the lady in blue scrubs said. "Glad to see you awake." She jostled a red bag onto a metal stand. The tube led to his arm. Ah, the pinching. "We got to you just in time. A little more of this and in a few days I imagine you'll feel much better."

A man in a suit stepped inside. Luke's heart launched into overdrive, and he stiffened. "Who are you?"

"I'm your protection detail, Mr. McGuire. Everything okay?"

The nurse nodded. "He's awake. That's a good thing."

The man nodded. "Will he be able to answer some questions in a few minutes?"

The nurse straightened. "I'll need to ask the doctor."

Movement at the door caused his heart to race until he spotted her beautiful face. Gabriella touched the suit's elbow. "It scared me when I didn't see you at the door."

The man winked at Gabriella. Luke exhaled. If Gabriella trusted the man, Luke probably didn't need to demand identification. "I'll wait outside," the agent said.

The nurse also smiled, as if in on a secret. "I'll let the doctor know you're awake."

In a split second the room cleared. Gabriella remained at the door. Two braids on either side pulled her hair away from her face. An array of small scratches covered her right temple. She wore a navy crocheted blouse. Her right hand cupped the area close to a hot-pink bandage wrapped around her elbow.

Luke tried to sit up.

She dropped her arm and reached out. "No, don't move. You've barely been out of surgery for an hour."

Surgery? He struggled to think of the last thing he remembered but drew a blank. Luke glanced at the bandage across his shoulder. They must have removed the bullet and stitched his muscles back together. At least he hoped they could do such a thing. Pink gauze wrapped around her arm, just above the elbow. "You're hurt."

She frowned. "No. They gave me the all clear an hour ago." She glanced at her elbow. "This? I just gave blood."

"No more allergic reaction?"

"Thankfully not." She gestured at the metal pole. "You're on your second transfusion," she whispered and looked away, blinking rapidly.

Luke tried to decipher what was happening but every word seemed stuck in a mind fog.

"They encouraged friends and family to donate," Gabriella said. Her eyes brightened. "Speaking of which, your family is on the way, on a plane as we speak. Everyone agreed it would be safest that way, since there is so much airport security already. They'll have escorts the moment they leave the airport."

"They are? They will?" Luke imagined the state of his current home. Probably not up to snuff to host his family right now. "Everyone?"

"Your parents plus your brother David and his wife, Aria. The rest of your relatives are staying where they are but have been assigned protection. I have plenty of room at the house if they need somewhere to stay," she added, as if she knew where his mind would track.

He remembered the seemingly frail lady wearing a nightgown in a black sedan, who'd pulled a gun on the mafia. The monitor confirmed the heart rate increase at the thought. "How's your aunt?"

Gabriella smiled softly. "Even now you're thinking of others. She'll be fine. Thanks to you."

Luke raised an eyebrow. "Please. I hardly did anything. Seems like the Lord turned every failed plan and attempt into success." He smirked. "Painful maybe, but we're alive so I call that a success."

If there was protection outside his door did that mean they were still in danger? The thought seemed to jar some of the sleepiness away.

Her laugh was light as she reached and touched his elbow. "That's a good way to describe it."

Her light touch shook the rest of his senses awake. He stifled a groan as the pain from his shoulder and hip pounded anew. "The escorts? The guy who said he's my detail…we're under protection?"

She sobered. "Yes. There is a chance of retribution or a possibility they may target one of our family members."

Luke gritted his teeth. It was one thing to put himself in danger, but his family? He reached for the bed remote and raised his bed further. He felt trapped in a cage. "What about my other brothers? James and Matt?"

Her eyes widened and she leaned forward. "You need to stay calm. Your mom wrote a list of every loved one she could think of." Gabriella swallowed. "Is there someone she…uh…wouldn't think of?"

Luke frowned and tried to take a deep breath. Even that hurt. "Um…no. Mom should've covered the bases. Except what if they target my receptionist or my contracted employees?"

Her fingers reached for his hand and squeezed. "I'm

sorry, Luke. I'll mention that to the agent." She straightened and as her hands slipped from his fingers, it jolted a memory.

Luke frowned. Had she told him she loved him? Or was it his imagination…a wishful dream? Even if she had, which was extremely unlikely, it could've been in the heat of the moment. He looked up to see her studying him. If it had been real, if she'd really said it, he would've gotten down on one knee right then and there.

She tilted her head, as if wondering what he was thinking. She'd probably run if she knew his thoughts. Because it wasn't a dream when she'd made it clear she didn't want to risk the friendship. He'd messed up once before, and he refused to do it again.

The nurse approached. "I'm sorry, but visitors need to wait outside. I got an alert his blood pressure increased. We need to monitor him and keep him relaxed. If any reactions to the transfusion were to take place, it would happen in the next fifteen minutes."

Gabriella paled. "I'll leave. Try not to worry about anything."

He leaned back. Easier said than done.

EIGHTEEN

Gabriella avoided the closet and her mother's room. Aunt Freddie had moved back into her old room in the house, with visits from a health care aide. The FBI took her mother's room for their headquarters…as well as the kitchen. The first couple of days after she'd left the hospital they'd kept her isolated, asking her questions that she could only assume they also asked Aunt Freddie.

After they seemed satisfied she'd told them all she knew, they spent their time searching the property for the mysterious coins and making sure the security teams were in place. Thankfully, they allowed her to get a new cell phone. But still, she and Aunt Freddie stayed separated. Gabriella didn't even know how to start a conversation, didn't know how to process what had happened. Almost two weeks had passed, and she still felt at a loss for words.

Gabriella flopped on her bed and pulled the corner of the quilt to her chest. The small frayed edges kept her fingers occupied as she relived telling Luke she loved him. Had he heard? Too little, too late? Especially now she had family ties to the mafia?

A slight knock at the doorway made her sit up on her

elbows. The door swung open, revealing Aunt Freddie dressed in a black-and-purple floral dress with a loose sweater jacket on top. Her silver hair sat in waves on top of her head, and if not for the fact that Gabriella knew they weren't related, she'd have imagined her own hair to look similar in fifty years.

"You okay, Aunt—" Her voice caught. She'd forever think of her aunt as Freddie and not Amalia, but now that she knew the truth...

Her aunt shuffled forward, and the light from the window highlighted her eyes. Recognition and sharp wit shined back at Gabriella. Except for a brief moment yesterday, she'd been lucid the past few days. "Call me Freddie," her aunt said. "It's been so long, and I don't want to remember the life that Amalia lived." Pain creased the area around her eyes. She reached a hand out.

Gabriella grabbed Aunt Freddie's hand. "Are you okay?"

Aunt Freddie released her and moved her hands to either side of Gabriella's face. "She wanted to tell you."

Her throat tightened at her aunt's words, and she avoided her aunt's piercing gaze. She didn't want to talk about her mother yet. It hurt too much. The lies, the—

"So many times," Aunt Freddie continued. "It's my fault she didn't, honey."

Gabriella stiffened. "What?"

"I'm ashamed, but you have to understand your Uncle Claudio was not a nice man." Her voice shook with a passion Gabriella didn't understand. Her hands drifted to Gabriella's shoulders. "He promised me if I ever left him, he'd find me and kill me." Aunt Freddie's eyes clouded over. "So when we left, I begged your mom never to tell you, even years later. I made her promise to wait until Claudio was gone. I'm sorry. I'm so sorry."

Gabriella's breath grew hot as her middle tightened, squeezed by an invisible corset of pain. What must it have been like to live in such fear? How would she have responded if she were her mother?

Aunt Freddie grabbed Gabriella's hands and sandwiched them between hers. "Your mother was the light of my life, Gabbie. When she came along—" Freddie choked out a sob "—I loved her like my own. Just like I love you. I hope you can forgive me, Gabriella."

"You were like a second mother to me," Gabriella whispered. "And to know how you tried to shield and protect and raise my mom...what you risked..." Gabriella closed her eyes, the tears burning against the lids. "How could I not?"

They clung to each other and cried, not only for the hurt from the past, but for the missing person in this conversation—her mother.

Three weeks later

Luke's shoulders sagged. Once the pain medications were no longer necessary, he'd struggled to sleep at night. Thoughts of revenge and hits out on his family or Gabriella plagued any shut-eye he managed to get. His phone vibrated.

FBI says threat over. No more guards needed.

Luke exhaled. Finally. That meant the grand jury had met today. The FBI had made both Gabriella and Luke write a list of any family members and loved ones the mafia would potentially target until the grand jury heard the case against them. It turned out to be an above-and-beyond gesture, as Luke and Gabriella weren't required to give testimony. The bag of evidence combined with the audio of Rodrigo was more than enough.

The phone and contacts they recovered on Benito's phone helped them recover the mole in the New Jersey FBI office who had helped keep tabs on the Boise FBI activity. Thankfully, every other agent had proved to be clean.

Luke rushed to his truck and headed over to see Gabriella. The FBI had wanted to keep them separated until the threat was neutralized. They were able to talk on the phone, but five weeks had been too long to go without seeing her.

He pressed the clicker, signaling to turn left. The black iron gate hung open to the Radcliffe Ranch. Luke's breath caught. He gunned the gas and stormed up the driveway until he spotted Gabriella, smiling and hugging her great-aunt.

Gabriella turned away from her aunt, focusing entirely on his truck. Luke pressed the brakes and pulled over to stop.

As he hopped out of the truck, his heart rate sped up, providing another reminder that so much of the blood pumping through his veins was no longer his own. Two transfusions later, his wounds still stung, but full recovery was imminent thanks to the hospital and a merciful God.

"What's wrong?" Gabriella called out, jogging to meet him.

"I wanted to ask you the same thing," Luke said. "The gate was open."

Gabriella reached for his hand and beamed. "We're no longer in danger. The grand jury met today. They're all put away. The Mirabella crime family is no more."

"Yes. I came as soon as I heard." He threw a thumb over his shoulder. "Still, it may not be the best idea to leave the gate open."

"Don't worry. The security systems are all back up and running thanks to the cash you found in the house." Gabriella pointed to the van pulling up the driveway. "And I only opened it when I knew they were on the way to pick up Aunt Freddie. She's ready to go back."

Luke matched her grin, knowing Gabriella wrestled with guilt and worry that she wasn't up to the task of caring for her aunt alone. They'd talked on the phone daily the past few weeks, and while Gabriella could manage her in the daytime during summer break, Aunt Freddie would wake up in the night and start roaming, unsure of where or who she was. It terrified Gabriella. "So she likes it at the assisted-living village?"

Gabriella nodded as Aunt Freddie approached. "I remember you," her aunt said.

Gabriella placed a hand on her aunt's back. "You remember *him*, Freddie?"

Aunt Freddie's gaze never left Luke. She held up a finger. "Oh, yes I do. Your mother was so impressed the way he treated you." Freddie put a hand on Gabriella's shoulder. "She never liked that *Thad*."

Gabriella rolled her eyes but laughed. "Yes, she made that clear. She had good instincts."

Luke found himself standing a little taller. He tried not to let it get to him, but Aunt Freddie's words puffed his chest. The fact her mother had mentioned him and Freddie remembered filled him with hope that was hard to tamp down.

"You here to talk sweetly to my Gabbie?" Aunt Freddie asked.

Luke flinched. How would Gabriella feel if he let Aunt Freddie know she preferred to be called by her full name? Probably not a good move, though. Gabriella blushed at her aunt's words, and even though Luke would've loved to talk to her sweetly, he remained determined to act as his brother and father had advised. "I'm actually here on business."

Gabriella's face fell. Luke didn't know how to interpret it. He thought she'd have been relieved. Maybe she'd had other offers from developers, or perhaps she'd found another way to keep the property. He could've kicked himself. His timing once again proved to be rotten.

Freddie's eyebrows rose. "Well, I've had my share of overhearing business talks for more than a lifetime." She hugged Gabriella around the shoulder. "You sure we're okay?" Aunt Freddie moved her shaking hands to either side of Gabriella's face.

"I'm sure," she answered and closed her eyes as if she knew what was coming.

Aunt Freddie kissed Gabriella's forehead. "God bless you, baby girl." She waved at the parked van behind them. A young man in a light brown jacket hopped out of the car and offered his arm. Freddie squeezed Luke's arm as she walked by. "I hope to see you again soon, young man."

"How are you today, Ms. Radcliffe?" the attendant asked as he led her away.

A rosy blush spread over Gabriella's face, complementing her brown eyes. He didn't realize he was staring, enjoying her beauty, until she looked down at her feet. "So you're here on business?"

The next part would be difficult. He cleared his throat. "You remember how I read your mother's diary?" He held his breath, waiting for the same reaction she'd displayed the last time he'd mentioned it.

"Yes. I actually had a chance to read it after the FBI helped me get the safe room back open." She grinned. "I feel a little sheepish about my reaction earlier, but I was afraid you might've found out something horrible about me. Like what if Mom vented about all my flaws?"

"I didn't learn anything about you that I didn't already know."

Her eyes widened, and Luke wanted to sprint and dive back into the lake to take cover. "Excuse me, I may need to call a crane to help remove this gigantic foot in my mouth."

She rolled her eyes. "Thankfully for you, I came to the same conclusion…you already knew all those things about me."

He laughed but lowered his chin. "I also knew your much more abundant list of positive traits, as well. Some that weren't mentioned."

She threw her shoulders back. "Didn't you say you wanted to talk business?"

Luke exhaled. For a moment there he thought she'd been flirting. Space. He needed to give her some space and focus on being her friend. She'd been clear in what she'd wanted. He'd admitted to his brother David he wasn't sure he was up to the job. The challenge of loving Gabriella while she thought of him only as a friend proved downright painful.

"If you want her in your life, it's the only way," David had replied. "You'll regret rushing love. Trust me."

"Yes, business," Luke said, harnessing himself to the present. "If you read your mom's diary, you also noticed she wrote a lot about her methodology for sand and gravel extraction. She kept it local to keep the value high but also took great effort in how she removed it… from an environmental point of view." He threw his hands up in the air. "Quite frankly, she was a genius."

Gabriella admired her surroundings. "You won't hear me arguing. She wanted to be a lifelong student. Believe it or not, she didn't have a college degree, but she was always taking online classes."

"That's where you get your love of learning."

Her eyes brightened as if she'd never thought of it before. "Probably."

"I've got two things to discuss. First, I insist you ask another developer for a bid—"

"We've already discussed this, Luke. If I feel the need, I will, but I don't need your insistence."

"You may change your mind, because I have a proposition that's different than we discussed. If I turned this land into a subdivision, it would be highly profitable, but it would destroy everything your mom built."

Her face fell. "I realized that before I approached you. Despite finding the money in the safe room—thank you again for proving it was legally earned—there's still not enough to maintain the property or take care of Aunt Freddie. Even if that wasn't an issue—"

"There's another option," he interrupted. "We could split the land into a luxury community." He spun around, pointing in all different directions. "The land suits itself to be split into four or five lots of ten to twenty acres each. There's plenty of room for a house on each, but if I added a conservation easement of a hundred acres, they wouldn't be allowed to destroy the water features. And, if the lots sell for the amount I'm thinking, you could keep your mom's house, if you wanted."

Gabriella rose on her tiptoes, her hands gripped together. "Can you really do that?"

Her enthusiasm proved to be contagious. "My dad and brother are both in the construction business. We brainstormed and researched and came up with this solution. The downside is it would take longer to be profitable."

She dropped back to her heels. "Oh. I see," she said softly.

"But if you're willing to consider my other proposition, that may not be a problem for you."

She crossed her arms across her chest. "Proposition?"

"As I was saying, your mom's work was genius. You inherited her business…"

"Yeah, but there's no way I could run it by myself. I don't know the first thing about—" She lifted an eyebrow as if realizing what he would say.

He flashed his best smile. "But I can."

She pursed her lips, as if replaying his words.

"Again, think about it. I have enough capital I could offer a down payment. That should at least help you for a while until—"

"No." She shook her head. "Absolutely not."

Her abrupt answer took the wind out of his sails. He

couldn't wipe the dumbfounded look off his face. His mind went blank on how to change the subject.

Gabriella jutted her hand out toward him. "Turn that down payment offer into a buy-in, and we'll be partners. Deal?"

"Partners?"

She nodded. "Yes. I know all my mom's contacts, and I'm a whiz at bookkeeping."

He smiled at her eagerness but hesitated, even though it made good business sense. What if she got a boyfriend? What if he couldn't handle just being friends?

The answer came to him quickly. He'd make the choice to act honorable in every situation, and the rest would be up to the Lord.

His hand joined hers. He relished her touch so much he dropped it. They'd need to keep handshaking to a minimum if he was to keep his distance. "Partners," he answered.

NINETEEN

Gabriella wanted to jump up and down at the day's turn of events. Her aunt seemed to be doing well and had proved eager to return to her own place at the assisted living village. Her financial needs for herself, her aunt and the property would be met.

And, last week, when she'd approached the local school district about possible openings, they offered her a job immediately. She hadn't realized the stellar reputation her nonprofit, and by association, she, enjoyed among local schools.

"Speaking of business, my executive director for the foundation was able to visit me yesterday."

Luke's eyebrows rose, and he shifted his feet. He sported slip-on leather loafers. Was he choosing dress shoes more suitable for running now? She examined him with new eyes. Instead of the designer jacket and dress pants, he sported a lightweight dark-blue-and-black flannel shirt, a thick leather belt and dark carpenter jeans. And he seemed more comfortable in his own skin. She hadn't thought it was possible to be even more attracted to him, but yet here she was.

"Oh? And how is she?" His question snapped Gabriella from her thoughts.

Ah-ha. She'd caught him. "I didn't say it was a she."

He shrugged. "You already know I nominated your organization for the grant. Give me credit for doing my homework."

"Oh, I'd say you did a lot more than homework."

He blew out a breath but didn't deny it, so Gabriella continued. "Maria told me she was able to track down the mafia money and return it to the lawyer. Except Maria had already allotted the money for a new tutoring site."

Luke nodded but avoided her gaze.

"Here's the amazing thing: this volunteer who she couldn't wait to tell me about was also the foundation's most valuable player during the school year. This volunteer preferred to keep his name off the foundation's service list, and he donated the exact amount needed to cover the returned money. What a guy, right?"

Luke cleared his throat. "That's great," he mumbled.

Gabriella playfully shoved his shoulder back. "Why didn't you tell me?"

His chagrined face sobered. "Haven't you ever heard the verse in Matthew about giving in secret? Can't a guy try to do a good thing without telling everyone?"

She reached for his hand and squeezed. She'd figured as much. And it meant the world to her that he gave his time and his money without expecting anything in return. "I can't fault that."

He shrugged. "You've always inspired me, you know that, Gabriella. And I… I'm good at math. I thought I could lend a hand, be of some help."

Gabriella's heart beat faster. It was true, all true, but she'd hoped there was something he'd omitted. Luke had always been a good man with a servant heart, yet she desperately wanted to hear there was more to it. "Is that all? No other reason?"

He looked up, and the way he looked at her drew her one step closer, without any thought. "There may have been," he answered.

As desperate as she was to hear him say the words that he'd done some of it for her, it wasn't fair to ask Luke to be vulnerable again when she'd yet to do the same. Well, she had, but Gabriella couldn't be certain he'd ever heard it.

A breeze brushed past her, swirling her hair around her shoulders and mercifully cooling her warm cheeks. "So, we're done with business?"

They stood in awkward silence for a moment, staring into each other's eyes. "As far as I can tell."

A family of swans crossed diagonally through the lake. She tracked their smooth progress as she gathered her courage. "I seem to remember once upon a time, before our lives were in danger, that you hoped to take me to dinner and catch up." She forced her voice to sound light even though her heart raced. It hadn't escaped her notice that their conversations had been strained ever since the hospital visit.

Luke met her eyes. He smiled wide for half a second until concern washed over his features. "Um. When you say go out to dinner…" He sighed. "I'm going to be straight with you, Gabriella. I'm determined to not rush you or push the friendship, but I'm also struggling." He looked down at his shoes. "I'm a driven person—"

She laughed at the understatement. "No news to me, Luke."

"So you know that once I've got my mind set on something, I have a hard time being patient. I don't want to mess us up… I mean our friendship. I guess I'm asking if you mean just as friends catching up or—"

"I said I love you." She blurted it out so fast she surprised herself.

He flinched, looked around as if she was speaking to someone else and jerked his gaze back to her.

She beamed, laughing. "I'm talking to you."

"When?" His eyes clouded with confusion.

She hated to remember the way his head hit the asphalt, the way his fingers had slipped from her grasp when the paramedics took him away. Her throat squeezed tight. "When you saved my life. It overwhelmed me. I'd missed your friendship so much…except, in my heart I knew I loved you much more than a friend."

"You said you loved me?"

It was as though he hadn't heard another word she'd said. Gabriella nodded and finally lifted her chin so she could stare into his blue eyes.

His mouth dropped. "And I missed it?"

Gabriella grabbed his hands. His response, his reaction made the doubt she'd had earlier scatter. She stepped closer, making sure he couldn't miss it this time. "I love you."

His lips pressed onto hers before she could prepare herself. He wrapped his arms around her waist and pulled her closer. He pulled back half an inch. "I love you, too."

Gabriella closed her eyes, soaking in the moment, and rested her head on his uninjured shoulder. She inhaled, and hints of pine and cedar with fresh citrus notes complemented the smells of the forest. He smelled like comfort, like…well, like Luke. And she never wanted to lose him again.

"I want you to know I'm all-in," he said. "I didn't want to scare you away, but I looked at some business opportunities in Oregon. Nothing for sure yet, but if I could get some work there we could see each other a little more during the school year."

She beamed. "And I didn't want to scare you, but I just accepted a teaching job here. I wanted to be closer to Aunt Freddie, but I'm all-in, too, Luke."

His hands pushed her back slightly. He bent his right knee, pain briefly crossing his features. He switched legs and dipped to the ground on his left knee. Her breath caught as he reached for her hands. "Gabriella, I…I know in my heart you are the one, and if you know, too…will you, would you, be my wife?" His eyes widened. "I mean not right this minute, I don't want to rush you, but if we both are committed—"

She laughed, moved her right hand from his grasp and caressed the side of his face, nodding wildly, her eyes suddenly blurry. "Yes," she whispered. "Yes."

Gabriella blinked. She didn't want to cry. She wanted to remember every moment in crystal clear color for years to come. She stepped back. Her mouth dropped. "Luke…"

He stood and pulled her into his arms. "Yes?" he asked softly.

"I want to always remember this…" She felt her eyes widen as her words triggered a realization.

Luke's arms stiffened and he inhaled sharply. "…to remember what God has done for us?"

She grinned. He understood her train of thought. She'd just figured out where her mom had hidden the coins. "Exactly."

"Are you sure you want to find out if we're right?" he asked.

Did she? She knew if she found the treasure, she'd likely find her father. Was she ready for that? Luke's support around her never wavered, much like her Father in Heaven. And if she could remember that…remember she would always be loved by her Heavenly Father no matter what, then she knew her answer. "Yes. I'm ready. Besides, we can always put the boulders back where they were if we're wrong."

"Agreed." He pulled out his phone. "I just need to make a phone call."

His brother responded immediately to his phone call. The rumble of the machine confirmed David was on his way with one of the machines Luke leased for his construction crew. Luke squeezed Gabriella's hand while the other hand held the shovel. "I think I need to buy this shovel from you, too," he muttered.

Gabriella cocked her head. "Sentimental, is it? I'm pretty sure it was the reason you ended up getting shot…the first time."

"Or the reason we were able to save the day. All how you look at things." He winked.

She flashed her wide smile. "Yet another reason I love you. Always focused on the positive."

His heart flipped. Would he ever get used to her saying those three little words? He pulled her closer and kissed her mouth.

At the sight of the skid-steer loader, he waved. His brother David filled the operating box, but a white pickup truck followed behind. "That's probably Aria."

Confident his brother had his sights set on Gabriella and him, they turned and walked in the direction of the boulders her mom had set up. Minutes later, Gabriella pointed to the third and fourth stones in the line of twelve. "Start in the middle," she said. "It's what I would do if I were Mom. And they are the biggest."

David's competent steering made short work of the boulders. He moved them about ten feet away from the river. Gabriella kept a sharp eye on the boulders. "I want to make sure we can put them back."

Aria hopped out of the pickup truck at the same time David exited the loader. She removed three shovels from the bed and walked their way. After introductions were made, Luke pointed to the area of the missing boulders. "Let's get digging. We have a treasure to find."

The four of them stood in a circle and stuck their shovels into the dry dirt. It only took three feet until they hit thick clay. "It's not looking good," David mumbled.

Gabriella's shoulders drooped, but she stuck her shovel in once more.

Dink!

Everyone froze, eyes wide, looking at each other. Gabriella pulled up the hunk of clay and pointed at a metallic box. Its green hue may have been from rust or… David leaned down and pulled on the top handle until it pulled away from its prison.

He set the box on top of the next boulder. Gabriella approached it cautiously. While it showed signs of aging, the green proved to be its original color.

David stepped away but gestured at it. "Looks like one of those ammo surplus boxes."

Gabriella touched the metallic latch surrounding the hinge and pried it loose. Her long fingers reached for the top handle and lifted. The squeak of metal against metal grated his nerves. The top flung open.

Luke, David and Aria took a step closer—four heads peering inside. Stacks and stacks of gold coins inside plastic tubes lined up vertically inside the box. Only the sound of birds chirping in the trees remained as they gawked at the sight.

The top coins all shone inside their plastic casings, untarnished by the years spent in the ammo box underground. Surrounding the border of each coin were roughly a couple dozen stars, and the woman in profile resembled the Statue of Liberty without the pointy crown. What Luke's dad would give to get his hands on these—legally, of course.

Gabriella reached for a small white card sandwiched between the tubes of coins and the side of the box. "I hadn't noticed that before," Luke commented.

She pulled it out. *If found please return to U.S. Mint C/O U.S. Treasury Agent Frank Wilson.*

Luke held his breath waiting for her response.

She clutched it to her chest and laughed. "I'm not Gabriella Mirabella, then. It doesn't rhyme."

"You know you can stay Gabriella Radcliffe, too," he reminded her.

She stared at the script. "I know." Her gaze slid to him. "But I think I like Gabriella McGuire the best."

Luke's chest rose, ready to burst with pride.

"What? Am I missing something?" David's outcry burst his bubble. Oh yeah, he hadn't filled his family in yet.

"Well, I was waiting until I got her a ring—"

Aria's squeal clearly indicated that wasn't necessary. Her outstretched arms embraced Gabriella. "Congratulations. I cannot wait for you to join this family. I mean, four boys at all the family gatherings. I'm telling you I've been waiting for another girl to join this family."

"Does Mom know?"

"Not yet. I just popped the question."

David reached a hand out and pulled Luke into a bear hug. "I think you're going to like marriage, bro." He patted him on the back. "Get in the habit of putting the toilet seat back down, and it'll be smooth sailing."

"David!" Aria slipped her hand through his elbow. "I think you and I should head back to the house and give these guys a moment. Your dad mentioned a messed-up safe room that could use our expertise."

David allowed her to lead him toward the white truck. "Okay, I need to tell Mom Luke's getting hitched."

"You can't tell Mom first," Luke objected.

"Oh, I'm telling her," David fired back.

Aria turned back and rolled her eyes for dramatic effect, then squeezed David's arm. "Stop trying to ruin their romantic moment with your teasing and come with me."

Gabriella laughed. "So that's what it's like to have brothers," she mused. She peeked back inside the green ammo box and gawked. "Can you imagine how much this is worth?"

"Probably best if we didn't think about it," Luke said. He wrapped his arms around her waist and kissed her softly. "Are you sure you're doing okay?"

"Yes. It's a tad overwhelming to think about meeting my father, but I'm hoping you'll go with me?" The question and the pleading in her eyes struck him to the core.

"I'd do anything for you." He needed her to know that, to rest on that.

She returned his kiss.

The sunshine glinted off the coins and reflected into his eyes. He squinted. "I will *treasure* this moment always." Gabriella giggled, and it only inspired Luke. "We'll look back on this in our *golden* years."

She rolled her eyes and pulled away, sliding her hands down his arms until they rested in his palms. "You make me laugh, Luke McGuire. But let's get one thing straight. If I groan or stop laughing at your jokes, it will never mean that I have stopped loving you." Her breath shuddered and her hands shook in his grasp. "And I do love you…so much."

Luke knew it, and he would never forget it. "And I love you, Gabriella. Knowing you has brought such a richness to my life, you have no idea." And he meant it.

Gabriella's head tilted back, and she let out a deep, contagious laugh he hoped he would hear for years to come. "Now that was good."

Luke reveled in the victory, although he'd never admit to the accidental joke. They turned to the house and strolled hand in hand toward their future. Without a doubt, it would be a good one.

* * * * *

Dear Reader,

I hope you enjoyed the adventure. I'm often inspired by stories in the news, both present and historical. Fellow writer Becky Avella told me about a mobster who had hidden in Idaho for years. My imagination ran wild. My questions and research led me to more fascinating news articles and potential scenarios for Gabriella to discover.

For me, this story is about forgiveness and God's timing. How many times have I rushed to make something happen, as Luke did with Gabriella in college, only to be told *no*? Sometimes I assume the answer will be *no* forever. And like Moses, when God finally says it's time, I don't want to go. Fear and doubt have set in. Sometimes we need a nudge to pick up that staff when it's time.

Until then, I hope—like Luke—to focus on whatever is good, whatever is right...

Blessings,
Heather Woodhaven

COMING NEXT MONTH FROM
Love Inspired® Suspense

Available May 3, 2016

TRUTH AND CONSEQUENCES
Rookie K-9 Unit • by Lenora Worth
Army medic David Evans has one goal: track down his late comrade's sister and fulfill his promise to look out for her. But he's shocked to find Whitney Godwin's a single mother and a K-9 rookie cop...with a drug ring's target on her back.

EMERGENCY RESPONSE
First Responders • by Susan Sleeman
When EMT Darcie Stevens is brutally attacked, she has no idea who is after her. But Detective Noah Lockhart is determined to find out who wants her dead—and keep her and the little girl she's caring for safe.

SEASIDE SECRETS
Pacific Coast Private Eyes • by Dana Mentink
Navy chaplain Angela Gallagher and army doctor Dan Blackwater are tied together by the tragedy that took the life of Angela's bodyguard. So when the fallen man's twin brother is in trouble, they rush to help him—and thrust themselves into danger.

PLAIN PROTECTOR • by Alison Stone
Social worker Sarah Gardner flees to an Amish community to escape her abusive ex-boyfriend. But when a stalker brings danger to her new home, can she trust deputy sheriff Nick Jennings to protect her, or will she need to run again?

TACTICAL RESCUE • by Maggie K. Black
When Rebecca Miles is kidnapped by criminals seeking the computer decryption program her stepbrother stole, she's rescued by her former sweetheart, special ops sergeant Zack Keats. But as they investigate her brother's treason, they realize that nothing is quite as it seems.

UNKNOWN ENEMY • by Michelle Karl
College professor Virginia Anderson won't let anything stop her from translating a set of ancient tablets—even attempts at blackmail that quickly turn deadly. But she'll need help from former Secret Service agent Colin Tapping to keep her alive long enough to succeed.

LOOK FOR THESE AND OTHER LOVE INSPIRED BOOKS WHEREVER BOOKS ARE SOLD, INCLUDING MOST BOOKSTORES, SUPERMARKETS, DISCOUNT STORES AND DRUGSTORES.

LISCNM0416

REQUEST YOUR FREE BOOKS!

2 FREE RIVETING INSPIRATIONAL NOVELS
PLUS 2 FREE MYSTERY GIFTS

Love Inspired
SUSPENSE
RIVETING INSPIRATIONAL ROMANCE